THE GOURMETS
OF GRANTVILLE

Bethanne Kim

Bethanne Kim
Visit my website at https://bethannekim.com/

Printed in the United States of America

First Printing: Aug 2021
1632, Inc.

eBook ISBN-13 978-1-956015-39-3
Trade Paperback ISBN-13 978-1-956015-40-9

CONTENTS

PART 1: 1631

Bethanne Kim

CHAPTER 1

September 1631

*I*t's the most wonderful time of the year....

As the door slammed shut behind her youngest, Bethel's smile dimmed. Today was the first day of the school year and Brent hadn't asked her for a thing. Her mind knew that her 'kid' gathering back-to-school supplies, getting his own haircut, picking out a first-day outfit, and even setting an alarm, getting up, eating breakfast (she hoped), and being out the door on time was a good thing. She and Raymond were supposed to want this as parents, and they did. Mostly. But her heart wanted to be *needed* and it didn't *feel* needed. When the kids were little, the first day of school felt like the most wonderful time of the year, exactly like the ad joked. With only one more 'first day of school' left for Brent and Bethel Ann already graduated, this year was bittersweet.

Raymond walked up behind her and caught her unawares in a strong hug. "Remember when we were expecting our Bethie? You wanted four kids and I wanted five. We ended up with two great ones. The Gardens are having that big first-day-of-school shindig

1

this morning. Why don't you call in and tell work you'll be in after lunch? Meet some new families and visit with old friends. I bet Linda Bartolli will be there. If she is, check and see if they have waterproof boots. Our not-so-little boy spent our last camping trip whining about his hurting."

She turned to face him, still holding tight, burying her head in his chest, her words barely audible. "You're right. It'll do me good. I do remember us wanting more kids and finding out we couldn't have them. Mom told me that we 'can't argue with what God chooses to give us' and I needed to 'stop whining about wanting more kids.' Not exactly a lot of sympathy there." Bethel suddenly pulled back and looked up at her husband. "Why are you still here? I'm not complaining, but this is the latest I've seen you home in the morning since we got stuck here."

He gently kissed her forehead. "I knew this morning would be hard for you, so I had John open the store. Bethel Ann will be down there too. They can't help anyone who has a prescription, but they can handle anything else. And right now, you need me more than anyone coming into the pharmacy is likely to need the small amount of medicine we still have in stock. If you put on your coat right now, I can walk partway with you."

"Let me guess: you'll be home late again." Raymond shrugged his agreement.

"I'll call you at dinner time with an update."

❊ ❊ ❊

It's the most wonderful time of the year....

Linda Bartolli smiled to herself and hummed the tune as she walked toward the Thuringen Gardens. *It truly is the most wonderful time of the year, for parents. Whoever came up with that ad a few years back certainly understood how we feel on the first day of school!*

And be of good cheer.... Linda lost the thread of the song as her ankle twisted, her foot slipped the rest of the way off the curb, and she crumpled toward a medium size mud puddle.

Splat.

She landed hard, enough of her weight on her hand to save her tailbone from damage. As her hand stopped sliding and she started picking pebbles out of it, her comments would have blistered the walls of an NCO club full of sergeants. *Not such a wonderful time now, is it, Linda? If Father Larry showed up now, that would make it perfect.* When a hand appeared in front of her face, for a moment, just one moment, she thought exactly that had happened, but there was no whiff of oil or auto maintenance about the feminine hand, and no priestly attire visible.

"Are you okay? *Ich heisse* Liesl Pfeiffer. You look pained."

Linda's attempted smile looked more like a grimace. "Okay, yeah. Great? No. But no lasting damage to anything but my pride. Nice to meet you. I'm Linda Bartolli, and I'm very relieved you aren't Father Larry. Having our priest overhear the organist swearing like that would be mortifying! Anyhow, I just saw my kids off to school for the first day of the year and I'm headed to the Gardens for the First Day of School Parent Shindig. I see your stack of first-day paperwork, so we can walk to the Gardens together. I'd rather not arrive with a wet butt from a mud puddle, but it's the closest place to clean these cuts and scrapes. I guess I'm Mama Wet Butt this year. "

Trying to piece together everything Linda had said with her limited English, they were halfway to the Gardens before the newcomer answered. "I am Liesl Pfeiffer. We came to Grantville early last month. They said our children must start the school today. The school is so big! I have worries for them, and much papers I don't understand." Liesl weakly waved the papers around, not sure at all what they wanted or how to fill them out, but very much not wanting to lose or damage them and possibly keep her children from the unexpected bounty a Grantville education seemed to provide. She had heard the classrooms were all heated and had seen for herself that there was plumbing, not outhouses.

Like most Germans, and unlike most English, she could do basic reading and writing. The forms seemed to be in German, but many of the word didn't make sense. What was a 'grade' and how should she know which one her child was in? Father, mother, and legal guardian all made sense, but why did they also need an 'emergency contact'? Why so many questions about health and diseases they had lived through?

"Every parent worries on their kids' first day of school. That's why the Gardens arranged their little get together, so parents can gather and talk for a bit." Linda looked around, seeing other down-timers clutching their own paperwork as they made their way to the Gardens. "Look around. You aren't the only one who needs help with paperwork. Ten to one, they bring in someone to help you all fill it out. By this time next week, you'll all be old pros! Your kids will be complaining about school lunches and homework, and you'll be dreading requests for help with homework in no time."

Liesl looked relieved, right up to the comment about lunches. "They don't bring food from home? Why complain about lunches? Are they not given enough food? Is food moldy or filled with bugs?"

Linda's shocked expression surprised Liesl. "Never! They would never allow such things to be fed to children! The kids usually don't like the taste, and they get tired of the same ten or fifteen choices. You can send lunch in with them, it's just usually easier to buy the school lunch and it's fairly cheap." When she finished, Linda sat, silently waiting, while a clearly shocked Liesl thought this over.

"Truly? They never, *ever* serve food with *any* mold or bugs? What do they do with those foods? With so many different meals, the children still complain?"

"Moldy or buggy food is thrown out, or composted, or otherwise gotten rid of." She didn't know how to explain kids not liking school food, so she didn't try.

Liesl decided she needed to wait before she asked any more questions about school. As they walked into the Gardens, she heard a song playing. She switched topics to ask about that instead. "I have a question not about school. What does this music mean? What is this 'most wonderful time of the year' they are singing about?"

Linda snickered a bit. "Playing *It's the Most Wonderful Time of the Year* on the first day of school is kind of a joke. It's a Christmas song. Kids think Christmas is the most wonderful day/time of the year. Parents, especially moms, are happy to see their kids go back to school and stop driving them nuts, so the start of school is 'the most wonderful time of the year' for a lot of parents, especially moms." Linda paused, briefly lost in thought. "It may sound like we are happy to get rid of the kids, but we are just as happy to see them hop off the bus and come home at the end of the day as we are to see them climb aboard and leave in the morning."

Liesl's face lit up. "I understand! For us, having the children back in school is wonderful. We aren't like the English. Our villages have schools for the children, but going to school is hard when the teacher has been killed or taken as a camp follower, the school burnt, and there is no food for anyone but soldiers. I think not having them 'under feet' will make doing things easier. But do adults not also like Christmas?"

"Of course we do! But it's a lot of work. Decorating, shopping for presents, making presents, shopping for food, baking cookies, wrapping gifts, cleaning the house before guests arrive, cutting down the tree, putting up the tree, decorating the tree…. There is so much to do! That can all be fun, too, it's just *a lot* to do in one month."

Grantville had already gotten Liesl so turned around with their talk of tolerating all religions, women being equal to men, and their other sometimes unbelievable ideas that she blurted out without thinking, "You do all those things? Just for the one day? You did not even mention church. Do you not go to church for Christmas?" As she finished speaking, Liesl realized what she had done and how much her foolish questions could cost her and her family, but it was too late to take back what she had said. Never, ever question another person's faith. Never. Unless the priest tells you to, then you always question it. But only if they tell you to. To make matters worse, another up-timer walked over and gave Linda a hug. She had clearly overheard. Liesl froze, too frightened to say anything more.

Now Linda was embarrassed. "We do, of course we do, but up-time Christmas tends to be more focused on family and friends, with a lot of parties, visits, traveling, and all kinds of things during the whole month of December, starting with our Thanksgiving feast the last Thursday in November. We have services every Sunday of Advent, then on Christmas Eve and Christmas Day, of course. The choir and organist prepare special music. As the organist at the Catholic church in town, I guess I think of that part of Christmas as my job, since it is, and not part of what everyone does for Christmas, since not everyone goes to church. The midnight service on Christmas Eve is my favorite of the year. The final song is sung by candlelight. A guitarist accompanies everyone singing 'Silent Night' as they leave. It's beautiful."

The other woman introduced herself. "Hi! I'm Bethel Little. I saw your expression when you finished talking and saw me, but you don't need to be afraid to ask those questions here. Most 'up-timers' are happy to answer questions, including ones about religion. No one in that stupid 250 Club or Irene Flannery, of course, but don't pay them any mind. The rest of us don't! If you're Catholic, you'll can't avoid meeting Mrs. Flannery at St. Mary's. My family are Christmas-and-Easter Methodists. That means we don't attend many services other than Christmas and Easter. We usually manage to put our butts in a pew for an extra service or two in December, but we spend a lot more time baking, going to parties, and making Christmas gifts."

A shadow passed over Bethel's face. "Well, not making gifts so much anymore. My kids think they are too grown-up and prefer shopping for them now. I miss having little kids." Liesl found it outrageous that kids said no to their parents and up-timers accepted it, but she kept her mouth shut. Grantville was their town. "I still bake a lot, though. The kids help sometimes, usually when it's something they want to eat. No one likes coming into the tax office, excuse me 'revenue collection', where I work but they get a little happier when I give them a treat. So, I bake."

Liesl cocked her head, feeling relieved that these strange women weren't angry. "Some things are the same everywhere. Especially not liking the tax office, but the Christmas traditions also. We have special food, too, for the holiday. Do you have gingerbread? *Und Glühwein? Und stollen?* Do you like ham or goose for Christmas dinner? What about sauces? I have so many questions about your food now!" Unlike religion, food was a safe topic. No one had been accused of heresy for saying ham was better than goose for Christmas dinner. At least, Liesl hadn't heard of that happening. Like any sane person, she avoided discussing the Inquisition, so it was possible they had decided eating ham, or goose, or not eating one of them, was a sign of heresy. But she was reasonably sure they hadn't.

Linda laughed. "It sounds like you may be a real foodie! We have gingerbread cookies but I'm not sure about the rest. I've never had time to learn more than basic cooking, despite my family's prodding, but I'm sure I can find some folks for you to talk shop with, so to speak. Right now, someone is about to speak to us all."

The forms were explained to the new down-timers while the up-timers met separately to learn about some new adult education classes in German and proposed changes to the schools. Everyone would be learning German, which was kind of obvious, and some of the students had already started Latin clubs in the middle and high schools.

When it finished, Linda found Liesl again. "I have to rush to work soon, but I want to make sure you meet some more parents before I leave. That's why the Gardens set this up for us! I see a few friendly faces, and a few lost looking faces. Let's go make some new friends!" Shy outside of the kitchen by nature, Liesl followed in Linda and Bethel's wake, meeting and greeting faster and more furiously than she had dreamed possible. She felt like she met more people in the next thirty-five minutes than had met in the rest of her life. Several, men and women alike, were avid cooks, all too happy to chat about their favorite recipes. Some went on and on about "barbequing" until they could break away to talk to someone new. One was so persistent in his diatribe on a "pit barbeque" that they faked needing to use the bathroom to escape. By the time Linda left for work, a new Cooking Club had formed itself. The first meeting was the next Monday evening at her house.

After years of pining for her childhood, when food wasn't scarce and the village wasn't poor or small, Liesl started to believe that maybe, just maybe, things were getting better. Maybe the wonderful fresh vegetables and herbs of the last month weren't such a brief pleasure. She could only hope to try this wondrous "barbeque" herself.

* * *

"Ladies, gentlemen," the down-timers all squirmed, uncomfortable at Linda addressing them that way, "I hate to ask you this since I barely know you, but the request comes from Rebecca and I want to help her. On her TV show last week, she asked for Germans to do a cooking show and a show on brewing beer. My son-in-law, Greg, told her I know some local people, up-timers and down-timers alike, who are starting a cooking club. Regular gourmets, according to him. If we do the show, they might be willing to buy the food we make on-air so whoever cooks that week will have a free dinner." Linda was wheedling and she knew it, but Greg had laid it on thick when he talked to her, so she was just passing the message along, really. Seeing the members looking back and forth at each other, uncertain, she kept talking. "I promise I'll come with you, if it helps! Janice Ambler, a high school teacher and the lady in charge of all this, will help too."

Bethel spoke first. "I'm in. Bethel Ann and Raymond are both working a lot and Brent is with his friends all the time. I'm not a gourmet cook, but this sounds fun!"

"Can we see the kitchen?" Everyone nodded at this. Up-timers were getting a reputation for an odd mania for constant cleaning, especially around food. They had all seen at least one up-time kitchen, but up-timers and down-timers alike wanted to see where they would be cooking before agreeing.

Linda let out a big breath she hadn't realized she was holding. "I'll be shocked if they won't agree to that. I bet Janice gives us a tour as soon as they know. The show will probably be taped in the old home ec kitchens, possibly in the middle school instead of the high school but the high school is where they broadcast from. There is a lot of interest, so they want to start taping asap. If we decide to do this, I think that makes us the official Grantville Cooking Club for sure! Let's come up with some ideas of what to cook and shopping lists so we are ready to go right away."

Gisela spoke. "Are we teaching up-timers or down-timers? If we are teaching up-timers, a nice vegetable stew. Even the most stubborn up-timers should accept that vegetable stew is mostly vegetables not meat. If Germans, they know how to cook so we need to show them how to use up-time stoves and adapt up-time recipes to have more vegetables. Like this 'meat loaf'. Who makes an entire loaf of meat?" Every down-timer nodded their agreement while the up-timers grinned a bit.

Linda answered. "Meatloaf actually has breadcrumbs and other things mixed in, so it isn't just meat. But, point taken, meatloaf would be a super expensive meal. Since we do like meat and we can't afford that much anymore, either, meatloaf *is* a good recipe to start with. Or meatballs, that's another good one. Do any of you make homemade pasta? My Nona made it and the store-bought crap can't touch hers."

The members looked around again, shrugging and shaking their heads. "Maybe if you find an Italian to join us? I hear they eat pasta."

Bethel couldn't tell who said that, but the point was valid. "Hmmm. My great-grandaunt Anna might be able to teach us all how to make homemade pasta. She grew up in Grantville, but she was born in Italy and learned to cook from her mama. Fresh spaghetti

11

with a garden-ripe tomato sauce and venison meatballs? Sign me up! Next fall, hopefully the tomato harvest is big enough to can a ton of tomato sauce!" Linda's stricken expression was almost comical. "Canning! We need to find a way to can things. We'll be lucky if there are any rings left anywhere for the jars by next tomato season, and rings will disappear soon enough, too."

Linda grinned. "That sounds like a perfect repayment for getting these TV classes started. I'll tell Greg to get his tech friends busy making us canning lids!"

The down-timers didn't know exactly what they were talking about, but they could tell a person horse-trading favors from a mile away. Whatever this 'canning' might be, Linda's son-in-law would find a solution for his mother-in-law, or he would not have a happy wife *or* a happy life come next summer.

CHAPTER 2

October 1631

Even after they knew they were stuck in 1631, Tina had allowed herself to hope for a miracle, to hope that somehow they could still help her. Still fix her heart. But there weren't any cardiothoracic surgeons in 1631. There wasn't even a real hospital. Sure, Grantville was building one, but that wasn't the same thing. Since no up-time cardiothoracic surgeon (or their tools) came through the Ring of Fire, the new hospital couldn't possibly have them. She needed to face the truth, and to do that, she had to be somewhere that felt totally, completely, safe. There was one place above all others that fit the bill, and so she was here, in the last pew, while her mom practiced for St. Mary's Sunday mass.

The familiar smell, the smooth wooden pew, the padded kneeler she idly flipped up and down with her feet. She smiled remembering crawling under the pews as a little girl, hiding while Brent tried to find her, while her mom practiced. Organ music was the background to her childhood. The feel of it sunk so deeply into her bones that vibrations from organ music soothed her at a primal level. So, she sat there, allowing the familiar sight of her mom practicing, repeating certain passages over and over until she had them perfect, light slanting in through the windows, to be the balm for her soul that they had always been.

After half an hour, her mom closed and locked the organ, then laid aside the boys tap shoes, sans taps, she always wore at the organ and bent to gather her music. Tina walked up to the organ and surprised Linda with a hug. "Hey kiddo! What are you doing here? Were you listening to me practice like you used to?"

Tina nodded, then closed her eyes briefly before telling her mom the bad news. "I saw the doctor today. They can't do anything for me. The short version is that I will keep feeling worse and being able to do less over the next few years, until one day I die. Greg went to the appointment with me, so he knows, but I needed some time to myself to think. This is when you always practiced, before work for you but after we left for school. It's nice to know some things haven't changed, even after the Ring of Fire 'changed everything'. I swear organ music was the first thing I heard in utero and that's why it's so calming for me!" Tina smiled at her mom, who had already heard that line more than a few times. "Seriously, I feel better now than I did when I came in. Hearing you play, hearing you practice, is a happy place for me."

Linda smiled at her daughter. "It doesn't bother you when I keep playing the same bit over and over to get it right?"

"It does not. Not even a little. It's part of the process. Soothing in its own way. It would feel like a private concert if you just went through all the pieces without trying to fix anything, and I like seeing

14

you practice. Anyone can see a concert. Hardly anyone sees rehearsals. When I am waiting for you in heaven, that is the picture of you I will hold in my heart: practicing the organ, completely focused on the music until nothing else exists around you." Linda's heart broke hearing her daughter talk about looking down at her from heaven at her mom instead of the other way around. "Not playing for services, not cooking dinner. Practicing, focused on making the music as perfect as you can before anyone else hears you play it. In that moment, for you, there is nothing beyond you and the music you are making."

Linda's daughter was a grown woman with her own husband and children. "One more song, and then I will walk you back to your house." She sat down at the piano and played their special song, the one she had played for Tina since she was a baby. As they walked down the front steps to the street, Linda hugged Tina and quietly said, "Love you, baby girl. You tell me what you need. Your dad and I will help you, Greg, and the kids get through this. You may be grown and a mama yourself, but you will always be my baby girl." For once, Tina simply hugged her back and didn't fuss over being called her baby girl.

* * *

Raymond dropped heavily down onto the kitchen chair. It was a heavy-duty model because he had destroyed three other, lesser chairs before Bethel realized he was never going to stop dropping down like that at the end of a long day. "I think we finally have it worked out. Vince and Lori were left up-time since they live out of town. The same with her folks. Her half-brothers Buck and Barry came through with their families, but they aren't any kin of Vince. Did you know he made her sign a pre-nup over the pharmacy? Can't blame him with that family of hers. We worked hard to keep this place running after we reopened it. He had a lot of blood, sweat, and tears in it before he ever met her. So, no claims from Lori's side.

"Both Vince's parents stayed up-time with him, and no one else left living on his ma's side. That leaves his dad's side. His first cousin John has the best claim. John's dad is the only one of Vince's aunts and uncles to come through, and he renounced his claim because he's 'too old to run a business'. In the whole Moss family, only those two came through.

"Now that he's been working with me for a few months, and we confirmed that no one else has a claim for Vince's half of the pharmacy, John is excited about becoming a pharmacist. He told me that him and his dad talked. They want me to commit to spending two years teaching John how to be a pharmacist and run the store. When that's done, they decided the right repayment is for me to own the land and the building, once it's done. We'll stay fifty-fifty partners in the business. I'll just own the land and building, nothing inside it. Even with vacancy rates having gone down so much in the last six months, Grantville real estate isn't exactly Manhattan real estate, and I'm going to have to put in *a lot* of hours to run the store, train John, learn down-time pharmaceuticals, and work the pharmacy. I'm not sure it's a fair deal for that much time and work. What do you think, Bethel?"

"Take the deal. We can't let the store close, too many people need it, and you can't run it by yourself. It's already been a strain and it's only been a few months. It'll just get worse. Honestly, you said it yourself, he already owns half. He doesn't have to give you anything for training him. He could sit there, doing nothing, and collect money. But he's doing the right thing and training to be a pharmacist like his uncle and you. Besides, what else will they pay you with? Money from John's 401K? It's a gift horse. Stop poking around in its mouth!" Bethel was genuinely happy about the deal. The house was lonely with Brent at school or with his friends, and Bethel Ann and Raymond at the pharmacy all the time. She hoped to see Raymond and Bethel Ann home a bit more.

November 1631

"Liesl! What a pleasure! What brings you into 'Bartolli's Surplus and Outdoor Supplies' today?" Linda and Liesl saw each other in passing at church most weeks and both were founding members and on-air personalities for the new Grantville Cooking Club and TV show. A few members still wanted to rename it the Grantville Gourmets, which sounded fancy and might scare off less-experienced cooks. Most members agreed that was exactly what they did *not* want to do. Now that they had a TV show named 'Grantville Cooking Club', the point had become moot. Even if they officially changed the name, everyone would know them as the Grantville Cooking Club.

"You missed our last meeting! A few children came home talking about 'scouts' and wanting to go camping with them. This led to talking about cooking over campfires outside. Then one of the up-timer women, I forget her name, but she promised to teach us how to make flaky pie crusts, said your store carries things just for cooking over fires." Liesl looked down at a note. "She said to ask for a 'pie iron', a 'Dutch oven', and 'hot dog sticks'. Do you still have any of these?"

"That is right up my alley! Yep, we've got 'em, but not a ton. You don't need hot dog sticks, otherwise known as a metal stick with a handle. Nothing fancier than that. You poke the end through a hot dog, marshmallow, or whatever and hold it over the fire. Sticks work just as well, but you have to clean and whittle them first so, up-time, people would buy hot dog sticks. Well, that and they worried that regular sticks were unsanitary. We are down to our last two pie irons here, but Phil and I must have a dozen squirreled away in our house. More than we need, at any rate. Now that you mention it, I should find a blacksmith to make more that we can sell." Linda grabbed a notepad from the counter and made a note to herself. "Dutch ovens, now, are something you probably already have, or something close to it. Phil already found someone out of Erfurt to sell those to us. Come with me and I'll show you."

A half hour later, they had gone through all the camp cooking gadgets on the shelves and were elbow-deep in a box of old stock and random parts in the back. Linda rocked back on her heels, holding an old mess kit in her hands. "I haven't seen one of these in years, not in a store anyway. Here, let me show you." She then proceeded to demonstrate that the mess kit included a small pot/bowl with a lid, frying pan with a folding handle, plate, and cup, along with a set of utensils that click together, all held in a closely fit cloth bag with a carry strap for easy transport.

Liesl picked up the pieces, examining them closely. "A tinsmith could make these. Many will buy them, if they are cheap. Walking, riding a horse, or in a cart, there is never enough space. This," she flipped the little set in the air and caught it, "would do nicely, and it doesn't even weigh much. How much for this one?" After a short haggle, both women were happy.

"If you find a tinsmith to make them, we'll buy them, Liesl. In fact, if you are willing to find a tinsmith and we make a business deal, you can have that genuine up-time mess kit as a finder's fee for helping us out. How do you know so much about what a tinsmith does? Was your father one?"

She grinned. "I will talk to my Andres about this before I agree to a deal. I will help you, but we need more time to set terms. *Vatti* is a butcher. The tinsmith's apprentice was cute boy. I spent too much time watching him work. *Vatti* spent too much time trying to make me stop. Then the apprentice became a journeyman and journeyed somewhere else." She got a sad look. "I heard his wife gave him a fine son their first year of marriage." After a moment she brightened again. "My Andres is a fine man, and we have strong boys. Not blacksmith strong, but strong for not-blacksmiths. Andres is a fine husband."

Linda couldn't help but laugh at that. "I get that. I know a lot of heavy metal music thanks to my high school crush. Playing some for you will be easier than trying to explain what heavy metal is, but he played in a 'garage band' and was sure he'd be a rock star someday.

He ended up working on a road crew doing construction outside Fairmont. Phil was a huge upgrade. Shoot! I totally forgot when you came in. I promised Phil I would start decorating the place for Christmas. I gotta go do that now."

"Christmas? In November?"

"Yeah, I know. It's early. All the stores started early up-time. It could be irritating, but this year, Phil and I need something happy and festive to distract us. A little bit of home." Linda shrugged. "We aren't using the Christmas lights, but the decorations will still…. Never mind. You'll see soon enough." Linda waved good-bye to Liesl before turning and rushing upstairs to the main storeroom to start pulling out Christmas decorations.

A few minutes later, Linda heard a tentative tapping that pushed the door open. Liesl walked in, already talking. "The Cooking Club ladies will be angry if I don't…." Seeing Linda puddled on the floor, tears streaming down her face, an open wooden box on the floor in front of her. Liesl stopped, unsure how to continue.

Linda's heartbreak was written clearly across every inch of her. "It's my daughter. For you, we have *brought* medicine and knowledge that saves lives. For us, we have *lost* medicine and knowledge that saves lives. One of those lives is my daughter's. She is a diabetic with a heart problem. Up-time, she was a nurse with medicine and surgery scheduled to repair her heart. Now?" She shrugged, tears still streaming down her cheeks. "The worst thing for a parent is to out-live their child. Up-time, it was rare and now I have to face the fact that Phil and I will bury Tina in the next few years. Already, she can do less work than she did when we got here now that her heart and diabetes medicine is gone."

Liesl hesitated a moment, then lowered herself next to Linda and engulfed her in a fierce hug. "My second son was Johan, born a year after Valentin. He was such a rosy, gentle baby, but never happy. Not one day. He cried, every day, as if he hurt. From the moment he was born, he cried in pain, but there was no injury. He cried himself to sleep. He cried when he woke. He cried when he pooped, and he cried when we cleaned him. The only time he didn't cry was while he nursed, but he would start again when he finished, and even while he nursed, his little face was crinkled like he hurt." For a few minutes, her tears joined Linda's as each wept for the pain of her own child. "He lived ten days. We don't know why the Lord took him from us so soon, or why He let our child be in pain for whole his short life, but burying him still hurt. The only comfort we have is that he was baptized and will meet us in heaven."

"Thank you." Linda's tears were slowing now. "Sometimes it just hits me so hard and can feel so lonely, like seeing that box of salt dough ornaments she made for the store when she was little. Before, everything 'wrong' with Tina was manageable and she had a lot of years ahead of her. Now those things will take her from us." Linda took a deep breath. "Enough of this. I am going to decorate for Christmas! It's much harder to be sad looking at Christmas decorations! You can tell the Cooking Club I will be at the next meeting with pie irons."

Liesl helped carry a few boxes downstairs, to be sure her new friend was 'okay' before leaving. Seeing all those boxes of Christmas decorations in the storeroom confirmed what most of the Germans suspected: up-timers are *verrückt*.

Thanksgiving 1631

Bethel gave the counter a final swipe, tossed the dishtowel in the laundry, and went out back to sit on the porch glider. Even after all these years, the view from the deck still calmed her right down to her soul. Raymond chuckled when he saw her shoot back up from the seat like she'd gotten an electric shock. "That old metal furniture is colder than a 250 Club reception for a Battle of the Crapper refugee. Hang on a sec and I'll move over so we can share this old afghan."

Snuggled into her husband of more than twenty years, stomachs full of Thanksgiving dinner, kids, cousins, and great-grandparents busy with their own things, Bethel noticed Raymond's head droop down, then the quiet snoring started. He did most things quietly. Since the Ring of Fire, most nights she didn't even hear him come into the house and climb into bed. Most morning she didn't hear him get up and leave. Part of her wanted to be mad that he was home so little, but she couldn't. Not knowing that he and Bethel Ann, her namesake daughter and his new apprentice pharmacist, were fighting so hard to find new medicines, then to refine and deliver them without dangerous guesswork. Her brain understanding didn't make her heart stop hurting, though.

The evening chill started cutting into her, but she wanted to stay there, nestled into her beloved, for as long as she could. The kids didn't need her anymore, but she knew he did, believed he did, at least, even if they didn't spend much time together anymore. She needed to find a way to talk to him. She needed more; her heart needed more. Her body might not think having more kids was a good idea, but her heart very definitely wanted them, and not grandkids.

She loved their eldest, Bethel Ann, but didn't want either of their kids to be forced to drop out of college like she did when she and Raymond found out her namesake daughter was on the way. Bethel and Raymond were barely past being kids themselves when Bethel Ann and then Brent were born. After the pharmacy was on its feet and they were ready to have a third, the doctors told them they had waited too long. Since they couldn't afford expensive medical treatments like in vitro, Raymond and Bethel had resigned themselves to not having any more kids. Thinking how to broach the subject, Bethel leaned forward, elbows on her thighs, head bowed in her hands.

"Just tell me."

Her head popped up. "You're awake."

Raymond's tone was dry. "Yes, I believe I am. When you look like that, you have something to discuss but you don't want to or don't know how to start. I can't spend enough time with you as it is. Let's not waste the time we do have with guessing games, so do us both a favor, and just say whatever you need to say."

She blurted. "I want more kids." Then Bethel blushed, embarrassed, and gave a pained smile. "That's not quite how I wanted it to come out."

Raymond's head tilted to the side. "Can't quite say I saw that one coming. I expected it to be about how I'm working too much, honestly."

"Well, yeah, but I get that. It sucks, but I understand. If you don't work, people die. Or, rather, people who could be saved die, so you work. Sticking to the topic, when we looked into adopting up-time there was so much paperwork and no guarantees and the expense…." Deep breath. "Now there are so many orphans, and almost no paperwork. I think it's only a page or two to adopt. Hardly more than you file when a kid is born. And the refugee center is full. Kids in other places are even worse off. And…."

"And stop." Raymond stood and held his hands out to her. "First, you don't need to convince me. Second, we are going inside where it's warm. Third, we will talk about what we want to do. I'm reasonably sure you don't want to adopt teenagers, since we already have two of those. I'm hoping you don't want an infant, because I *really* don't want to learn about down-time diaper changing and potty training."

"Wuss."

"Guilty as charged. But it gives you cover so you don't have to 'fess up to not wanting to deal with it yourself. So that leaves preschoolers, elementary school, and possibly middle school, if you really want to go that route. We need to talk to the kids before we do this. Having little kids in the house will be a big change for them, too, especially Brent. There will always be orphans. We can take the time to do this right." Joy radiated from a very relieved Bethel. "I'd say we need to look at our finances, but we are so much better off than most people born here and now that I have been feeling guilty myself about not opening our home more to those in need. Even if it forces us to tighten our belts a bit, it's worth it."

"Tighten your belts a bit for what that's 'worth it'?" Grannie B and Grandpa Eli weren't as asleep as they appeared, sitting in two old recliners. Before Bethel and Raymond formed a coherent answer, Bethel Ann, Brent, Krystal, and Sam all appeared from various parts of the main floor.

Sam spoke. "Don't stand there looking at each other. Inquiring family members want to know. Spill." Sam figured he was only repeating Grannie B's question, so he could be a little nosy.

"You mean nosy."

"Aunt Bethel, you are stalling."

Sigh. "Fine. Uncle Raymond, your dad," looking at their kids, "and I were talking about maybe looking into adopting a down-time orphan. Maybe more than one? We're not sure. Not babies, but not teenagers either. We just barely started talking about *possibly* adopting five minutes ago, and that's as far as we had gotten."

Grandpa Eli looked around the room, then at his wife. She nodded her agreement and he got both their coats. As she started buttoning her coat, Grannie B spoke to Krystal and Sam. "What are you waiting for? You two are taking us home so these four can talk. You better shake your tailfeathers or us old coots will beat you out the door!" Grannie B's demonstration of shaking her own tailfeathers completely broke the tension that had started to build in the room.

25

CHAPTER 3

First Sunday in Advent, 1631

"With so many decorations in your house, why do up-timers not have an Advent wreath in your house like the church has?" Anna Maria Schneider verh. Schulte asked Irene Flannery as they walked out the door after mass. Unlike a lot of people, she wasn't afraid of the legendarily cranky old lady. She had known a lot of cranky old ladies, and Irene Flannery, at least, was unarmed.

"I don't know, but I have never seen one in a home. Perhaps if more people *did* have Advent wreaths in their homes, then *some people* might think more about the baby Jesus and less about the Santa Claus." Irene sniffed her disdain for *those people*, which included almost everyone except herself and maybe (possibly) Father Mazzare. "Can you make one yourself? And could you teach other people how to make one?" When a bemused Anna Maria nodded yes to both, Mrs. Flannery propelled her toward their priest. "Father, this young woman would like to teach a class on making an advent wreath for your home."

Seeing Anna Maria's shocked, deer-in-the-headlights expression, and knowing Irene Flannery quite well, the good father took a moment to frame his reply. "That's a splendid idea, Mrs. Flannery! Of course, you know how busy we are trying to help the refugees with their housing and other needs, so I don't think we could have a class here at St. Mary's this year. *Frau* Schneider, what do you think about having a small class in Mrs. Flannery's house, since it was her idea? I know the old Reed house where you live is quite a bit more crowded than Mrs. Flannery's house, at the moment. If your class goes well, you can move it here next year and teach a larger group or even several groups, if you like." Father Larry knew full well that Irene Flannery barely let people in her house when something absolutely needed an emergency repair *right now*. They were all still amazed that having refugees move in the previous summer hadn't given her a literal stroke. Allowing a group of unknown women in for a crafting class simply would not happen.

Anna Maria's relief was palpable when Mrs. Flannery sniffed again, then turned and left, muttering to herself as she walked away, but she kept thinking about Mrs. Flannery's suggestion all afternoon. Before dinner, she spoke to Krystal since they were living in what was effectively her house. At dinner, she spoke to everyone in the house. "*Frau* Flannery suggested I teach a class on making an Advent wreath. I have decided I will do this. I spoke to Krystal and I will have the class here, at the dining table."

Everyone started talking at once, asking for more details and worrying how they might be affected. Anna Maria's husband Heinrich finally shushed everyone else and started asking his questions. When will the classes be? (Mid-morning on Saturday, possibly on weekday evenings after dinner or mid-morning, if enough women are interested to do more classes.) Will any of them be at mealtimes? (Semi-patient pause while he mentally reviewed the previous answer.) Will people pay to take the class? (For the first one while she's still learning what to do, only enough to cover any costs, which there shouldn't be any of. After that, a small fee per student.) Will it cost the family anything? (No, it should make money.)

Their daughter Agatha asked the last, and possibly biggest, question. "Why are you doing this, *Mutti*?"

None of them were sure what to expect, but Anna Maria's answer wasn't it. "I'm not entirely sure. After my conversation with *Frau* Flannery and Father Mazzare this morning, I couldn't get the idea out of my head. I have heard up-timer women mention 'crafting' as a thing they miss. The word doesn't make much sense the way they use it, but it seems to mean they like to make small decorative items for themselves or their house, or sometimes bigger things like clothing. If I can find a way to teach them 'crafting 'of down-time things, I can perhaps make a small business. If I can find a way to bring this up-time crafting craze to down-timers, then I can perhaps make a *large* business."

Heinrich gave his wife a considering look. "Have these up-timers convinced you that *every* woman needs to own a business? Where do the rest of us fit into your future business empire?"

"Don't you worry, husband! This would take all of us! You, most of all, can make many things to sell them, if you wanted, like sewing hoops. Or you could teach men man-crafting things like simple woodworking since even the Guilds don't bother people too much about what they make for their own personal use, if they don't try to sell anything. But that is for later. For now, I will teach one class, for free, to see if women have interest, and to see if I can teach. If I cannot teach, then we would need to hire a teacher and we cannot pay a teacher, so that would be an end to it."

Sam had been sitting quietly, listening to them. "You are going to be so rich." Seeing the down-timers confusion, he continued, "Seriously, rich. My mom liked to knit. She filled the spare bedroom closet with nothing but yarn waiting for the perfect project, and more pattern books than I care to remember. Some of that yarn waited for years, then she found 'the right thing' to use it for. Anyone who got into crafting seemed to have at least one closet full of stuff for their preferred craft, and a bunch of pattern books, and they were always buying more." The down-timers looked skeptical at the thought of an entire closet of perfectly good yarn just sitting there, unused, for years, but everyone knew up-timers were *verrückt*.

Krystal chimed in, "He's totally right. Most called it their 'stash'. But since his mom had to work all the time, she couldn't join any clubs. My nana got my mom to join a scrapbooking club. You do *not* want to know how much stuff scrapbookers collected, and how weird those little things could be. Nana had this giant collection of shaped paper punches, little gadgets that made holes a certain shape in pieces of paper to make them fancier. Back to the point, if you have all the materials and are ready to go into business when the worst worries of war, famine, and our safety are over, he's right. You are going to be *so* rich."

The next morning, Anna Maria stopped in at the rectory and left word that she would teach up to four women how to make wreaths, if she could get one more to be her assistant. They could fit six people at the dining table in the Reed house. To everyone's surprise, Mrs. Flannery insisted on assisting her. Anna Maria had never taught a class before, but Mrs. Flannery had decades of teaching experience and took it upon herself to teach her how to be a teacher. Despite her curmudgeonly exterior (and interior), she was quite skilled at helping young teachers become confident and competent in the classroom, and not only because it was a legitimate excuse for bossing them around. This was teaching crafts, but Mrs. Flannery was a seamstress and teaching was very much in what passed for a happy place for her, doubly so when teaching crafts. She was determined to make Anna Maria a competent teacher whether teaching was a happy place for her or not.

By the end of the first wreath-making class, each of Anna Maria's students had an Advent wreath and Anna Maria was determined to make this into a business, when things calmed down enough. *Frau* Flannery was as prickly as everyone said, but she was also an experienced teacher and Anna Maria could handle prickly easily enough. The more she thought about the ribbon wreath on the Reed's front door, the tree skirt, the stockings, and all the other homemade decorations she had seen in the houses, the more excited she became about making this a business. She managed to fit in four more Advent wreath-making classes before Christmas. After the struggles of the war years and a lifetime doing jobs they didn't enjoy, the profits from a job Anna Maria genuinely enjoyed made her and Heinrich both extremely happy.

Until things settled down enough that women had time for crafting classes, Anna Maria would learn as much as she could of up-time crafts. As soon as there was a *Kristkindlmarkt* in Grantville, she would start selling her wares and getting people excited to take her classes.

* * *

Gisela finished the broadcast. "Thank you for joining us again this week! We hope everyone enjoyed learning how to make 'salt dough ornaments' for your house and your tree. If you want to see some genuine up-time salt-dough ornaments, the ones made by the owners of 'Bartolli's Surplus and Outdoor Supplies' were the inspiration for this episode. Next week, we will make mashed potatoes and gravy. The last TV show of the Grantville Cooking Club for 1631 will be making *Glüwein* for the up-timers in our audience. Remember, there won't be a new show between Christmas and New Year's Eve! We will be home enjoying our families and hope you will be enjoying yours!"

Janice held out her hand in a 'hold' sign, then said, "And you're off the air. Your show is fantastic. I hear 'The Cooking Club Show' is must-see TV for many women, and more than a few men. We have a several gents who would like to share their barbeque skills in a future episode, presumably in the spring so no one gets frostbite filming outside."

"Thank you. I don't know why it would need to be filmed outside, but I would also prefer to wait until warmer weather if something must be filmed outside. Central heating is a good thing. A very, very good thing."

"Ah, well, that isn't the only reason I'm here." Janice cleared her throat. "Lyle Kindred of *The Grantville Times* has been talking to us. He needs some regular features for his paper since some of the old standards like sports coverage are gone. He'd like to add a weekly feature of the Grantville Cooking Club recipes." Gisela and Tina were the featured presenters that day. Liesl was there to help, and Linda was there moming her daughter, for which Tina felt almost equal amounts of irritation and thankfulness. "Thoughts? Ideas? Feelings? Anything at all?"

Both down-timers looked lost at the idea. Since the words of women were rarely published in any form, much less sought out to be published, they had never in their wildest dreams considered such a thing. Having pushed herself physically to tape the episode, Tina was tuckered, leaving Linda to answer. "The Club will need to talk about it, but I think a regular newspaper column is a fabulous idea. Does Lyle just want recipes or is he looking for a bit of description, an introductory paragraph or two? Does he also want the segments on things like best uses for a microwave?"

Janice threw up her hands in a clear "stop!" motion. "I'm only the messenger! It sounds like you are generally willing. One of you should stop by the *Times* or call and meet with Lyle to iron out the details."

Christmas Day 1631

With the speechifying and sermonizing done, the whole Reed clan headed from the high school football field toward the cafeteria. Grannie B broke their silence. "That Reverend Jones spoke so well it almost made me wish I'd gone to church with you a few more times these last years, Eli. Didn't know the Methodists had such powerful speakers. 'Course, my parents would roll over in their graves if I had gone. But I like what he said just now."

Sam looked thoughtful. "What did you think of Father Mazzare's sermon, Grannie B?"

Looking embarrassed, she admitted the truth. "I couldn't understand most of what he said. A few words here and there, but I never learned Latin. Before Vatican II, I followed along with the words but didn't understand most of 'em. That was a long time ago, even to an old coot like your great-grandma!" That got the expected chuckles.

Sam nodded. "Yeah, that's about how I did. I almost understood a few sentences, but by the time I worked out one section, Father Mazzare had moved on far enough that I couldn't understand his speech."

Grandpa Eli looked more astonished than Grannie B. "When did you learn Latin, boy?"

"They have classes at the high school now. Not everyone is studying Latin, but I wanted to learn it up-time to help with science classes, if I ever went to college. When I found out they were planning classes here and now, I got on the list early to make sure I got one of the spots. I have friends who speak fluently so they are helping me study." Embarrassed by the attention, he changed the subject back to the Christmas sermons they had just heard. "Your priest seemed to do a good job, Grannie B. What do you think if I come to mass with you a few times and you come to church with me a few times? That way things will even out with your parents, and I can work on my Latin!"

Watching the kids getting antsier with every passing minute, Grandpa Eli recognized the problem. "You youngsters run ahead and find your friends while the rest of us follow at a more sedate pace." He had barely finished when they zoomed off.

Bethel watched them run ahead. "It makes me wonder a bit. All those years with all that worry about gifts and Santa and look at them this year. No Santa, not many gifts, and they are still having a grand time."

Mike Stearns surprised them when he spoke. "Nothing like being stalked by the horsemen of the apocalypse, or seeing them in the general area, to make folks appreciate an old-fashioned church-focused Christmas. What? You think just because I got elected, I don't talk to regular folks anymore?"

Grannie B recovered herself first. "Michael Stearns, that was a lovely program. Wish I could've understood the first two speaking, but Reverend Jones' sermon was one to reprint and keep a copy of."

Rebecca Abrabanel spoke. "I can't do the Rabbi's sermon justice so I won't try, but part of the first sermon was thanking God for providing *Juden* with a safe place where we can live and worship freely. This is truly as much a miracle for us as the actual Ring of Fire, and as hard to believe as the other miracles we see every day, living here." No one could add anything to that.

After a minute of silent walking, Mike broke the silence. "I want to get to the cafeteria before the kids eat all the potato chips, so you'll excuse us if Rebecca and I speed up a bit. Enjoy the party!"

As they walked away, Grannie B's eyes lit up. "Potato chips? Truly? Your Grandpa Eli and I heard people talking about them the last few days but they're old folks like us. I thought that was just a rumor."

They joined the cafeteria line right behind Linda Bartolli and her family. "The choices are plain or plain. Salted, of course, but plain nonetheless." They moved forward a few steps. "It looks like down-timers are enjoying them. What do you think about having the Cooking Club get the recipe and experiment with flavoring? Phil likes sour cream and onion, but I prefer barbeque. Well, my actual favorites are some specialty chips ones from Baltimore with a crab on the package. They don't taste like crab, but we don't have whatever the seasoning was, so I'm going to lobby for barbeque flavored chips. *If* I can get the Cooking Club to agree to try."

Janice Ambler was passing by and heard the comments. "I support this! I'm a huge fan of barbeque myself. There aren't many potatoes available, though, so you may have to stick to making one small batch. Knowing how few potatoes we have, and how zealously Willie Ray Hudson is guarding them as seed potatoes, I would say there is zero chance of you getting any for cooking, but a segment showing how to make potato chips at home might push some farmers into the 'willing to plant 'em' category. Since Willie Ray says we need every farmer we can get planting potatoes, that may convince him to let you have a few. Grantville has a lot of mouths to feed these days. Giving those kids all the potatoes they needed to make enough chips for everyone at the Christmas party practically put Willie Ray in physical pain. That means you shouldn't plan to make anything else with potatoes before the first batch comes out of the ground, possibly even the second. Make sure that's clear to everyone: we have to grow them before they can eat them. Then introduce mashed potatoes for Thanksgiving."

Bethanne Kim

PART 2: 1632

Bethanne Kim

CHAPTER 4

January 1632

K rystal answered a knock at the front door, surprised to find Irene Flannery carrying what appeared to be two reusable grocery bags filled with books and folders. "Come in, Mrs. Flannery. What brings you here?"

"I would like to speak with Anna Maria, please. I have brought some things for her. I will wait here while you find her for me." With that, Mrs. Flannery removed her coat, sat on the sofa, and began removing things from her bag. "What are you looking at? I'm an old lady. I will die right here on your sofa before you get her at this rate. Go find her. Now."

Anna Maria was equally confused when Krystal came into the kitchen. "Anna Maria, I don't know exactly what she wants, but Mrs. Flannery is asking for you. She brought a bunch of books with her so whatever she wants might take a little while. I'll help Gisela finish dinner while you talk to her." Krystal made shooing motions to tell the woman more than twice her age, who had faced literal armies, to go face Irene Flannery. Anna Maria wasn't afraid of cranky old ladies, but she didn't relish being called in front of one for mysterious reasons.

"Hmm. Took you long enough." Mrs. Flannery gestured to a pile of pamphlets, books, and other media spread out on the table. "Before God sent us back here, being eighty years old was not so terrible. Not easy, but doctors fixed a lot that we must suffer with now. Without my arthritis medicine, I feel my age. I was a schoolteacher for many years. After we came back here, the school took some of my old books and teaching materials, but not all of them. Since I will not be a teacher again and may not live many more years, I am giving you these books and papers on how to teach, the ones the school thought were 'too old', like me. They are not complicated English so you should be able to read them soon enough if you can't now.

"Experience will teach you most of what you need, but these can help you improve. It's easier to have a bit of a guide to make lesson plans and that sort of thing. Keep the bags. I have others. No need to have these things cluttering up my house. Once we both agree you have the knack of it, I want you to teach others to be teachers so lots of people can learn crafting and other things."

This was a lot for Anna Maria to take in. She opted to go with the obvious point. "But I am not a teacher."

Snort. "Of course you are. You are teaching women crafting. Same principles as teaching kids in school, just more hands-on than history or reading."

"Thank you, but this is too much. Books are valuable, and the bags! This should go to your family or...."

Mrs. Flannery snorted. "You can finish 'or friends'. The only friend I have had in decades is Barbara Reed, and she's older than I am. I'm the only one left in my family. My husband's family doesn't need, or want, anything from me. The last time I tried to do something nice for them was nearly twenty years ago when their Fran got married, and they turned me down, flat, when I offered to make her wedding gown, as if I wasn't good enough for her. These are my books and papers to do with as I please, and I please to give them to you so you can teach crafts, then teach others to teach crafting. So. That's settled."

Anna Maria was overwhelmed by this generosity, especially given that everyone knew Mrs. Flannery wasn't a giving person. "Thank you. But please, why? Why me?"

"My Nana used to knit, and garden. It's almost the only thing I remember about her. If she wasn't cooking, cleaning, gardening, or somehow taking care of the family, she was knitting. She had a rocking chair in the store with a basket for her knitting. No one else ever sat there. I still have her knitting needles. I remember her looking at sewing machines in the catalogs, so I think she wanted to sew but without a sewing machine, sewing took a long time and was hard on your eyes. Back then, sewing machines were still new and far too expensive for most of us in West Virginia.

"My Mama loved gardening and herbs, too. She tried to teach me about the herbs she and Nana had planted, but I was young and uninterested back then. I only liked pretty flowers, like roses, not practical ones like vegetables and herbs. Anyway, in the winter, after Nana passed, Mama used those same knitting needles to knit us things and she embroidered some of my dresses to make them just so.

"Before he died, my Papa collected can labels. He started wallpapering our extra bedroom with them. He told me that his dad collected labels that fell off cans in our little general store, almost by accident. After a while, they turned into a collection with so many that he needed to find something to do with them. Since Mama was nattering at him to paint the room, he told her he would wallpaper it. She was not so happy when she figured out he was using can labels and the project might take years to finish. Once he died, she put proper wallpaper over all those old can labels. They are still there under the layers of wallpaper in that room." The more Mrs. Flannery talked, the more confused Anna Maria was, although she kept nodding as if she understood.

"After Papa died, Mama used some of her money to buy a genuine Singer Featherweight and start taking sewing and home economics correspondence courses from Mary Brooks Picken. You wouldn't have heard of her, but she was quite famous when I was young. Mama and I did the courses together, and Mama took in mending to make ends meet. When she died a few years later, I kept taking the courses. By then, I had finished my training and started working as a schoolteacher. So, you see, my family are crafters, all of us in our own ways, including Papa. Through all my years as a teacher, I have seen how many young people are made happy by their own crafting, even when the quality was not up to my family standards."

Irene was silent for a minute. "I would very much like to see the crafts my family loved become known in the here and now, and not limited to a few rich people. When you taught the ladies how to make advent wreaths, you cared. Crafting is new for you, but I think it is something you can love, and you can teach that love to others. I have a pretty fair idea what people think of me, and why. I have never been an easy person, but I like to believe I have been a fair person. You have little, even less than the coal mining families I grew up around and taught. I used to make jackets for some of the children who didn't have a jacket to wear at all. They didn't know I sewed them, though. The jackets just appeared in the closet with their names pinned on one day." She reached down and ran her hand across the books in a gentle caress. "These books helped me learn to be a teacher. To teach those children, and to care for them as best I could, especially in the years before we had social workers. Over the years, I lent these books to others and helped them become teachers. Now, I have no more use for them, and I am giving them to you so you can become not only a teacher, but you can, in turn, teach others to be teachers."

Stunned, all Anna Maria could do was nod.

"There is one other reason. Sam said you may start a business. When I was young, there weren't always laws saying women couldn't do things, but they couldn't do them all the same. There was no law that said I couldn't run a store or that my Mama couldn't, but the men would've made it hard to buy things, to hire people, to get fair prices for goods. That's why she closed the family store and I became a teacher. If you do this business, you can help other women start businesses and earn money for their own families. There are hard choices no woman, no person, should ever have to make, and being able to earn your own money, maybe own a business, helps with some of them." The silence stretched on after Mrs. Flannery stopped speaking. After a minute, she stood up to leave. "If I find other things that may be of use to you, I will send them over with Sam or leave them for you at St. Mary's."

Anna Maria couldn't think of anything to say other than thank you, and that didn't feel like enough, so she remained silent, head bowed in thanks. She looked up as Irene Flannery bundled herself into her winter clothing and grabbed her tote bag. "Young lady, take it from an old curmudgeon, chances like this don't come twice. Make the most of it." Having said her piece, a weight lifted from her, almost visibly, leaving Irene Flannery lighter and a bit more at peace than she had been in decades as made her way home.

✻ ✻ ✻

Everyone in the Grantville Cooking Club had a turn being on TV. Linda hated being in the spotlight and had avoided hosting the show so far, but her luck had run out. Tonight, she was the up-timer half of the hosting duo. At least she really did love potato chips. "I don't know about our viewing audience, but the members of the Grantville Cooking Club all enjoyed the potato chips we tried at Christmas. We have it on good authority that they fried them, but we will be baking our potato chips because we won't use cooking oil that freely."

Liesl picked up. "After some experiments, we can now make baked potato chips, carrot chips, and other veggie chips. Done this way, making potato chips is not so different from dehydrating fruit like apples and pears. For making potato chips, *Frau* Bartoli brought something called a 'mandolin', which is a small board that holds a knife edge with a slit beside it. Slide a vegetable across it and you can rapidly cut them into whatever size you want. Many of us go as quickly with a knife, but this multipurpose gadget seems far more useful than some of their gadgets. Perhaps there are some among our viewers who will start making and selling these 'mandolins'! Until then, you will need to use a knife for the same thing."

Linda spoke. "We will explore a few more up-time favorites that use potatoes later in the year, after the first crop has come in. If you are a farmer and don't have your seed potatoes yet, now is the time to ask for them, before they run out. Because most of the potatoes are being kept as a seed crop, we will only make a small batch of potato chips in this show, then we'll switch to making chips from carrots and other common root vegetables."

Liesl finished the opening spiel. "Finally, we will be talking about how up-timers handle kitchen fires. We can all see that they have kitchens right inside their houses, no matter how large the house is, but have no fear of a cooking fire burning their house down. These wonderful stoves and microwaves are a key part of that, but not the only part. In fact, they don't even consider the stove part of preventing home fires! No, I know it's hard to believe, but it's true. Even the oldest among them can't remember cooking over an open fire in their home. They *really* don't think of kitchens the same way we do."

"Now, let's get cooking!"

February 1632

Bethel Little plopped down at the table in her grandparents' old home, the one her niece Krystal and nephew Sam (cousins, not siblings) lived in now. "I miss hotdogs. The sausages here and now are good, but the buns are all wrong. Hamburger buns are even worse! I wish someone could figure out a way to bake those."

Bethel, Krystal, and Sam glanced at each and said, in unison, "If wishes were fishes!" Anna Maria and her daughters Agatha and Gisela looked at them like they had lost their minds.

Krystal laughed, then explained. "It's something Grannie B always says. No one knows quite why, but she clearly likes the expression. It just means wishing for something doesn't make it happen."

With that clarified, Gisela had a thoughtful expression. After a minute, she spoke up. "Do you have a recipe? Or can you help me find one? They could be eaten with *wurst*. The Grantville Cooking Club would like to try making these hot dog buns, I am sure, possibly put them on the TV show, if all goes well. I can try to sell some to the Thuringen Gardens. They always like down-time/up-time food."

Sam threw his hands up in the air, wordlessly saying, "Not me—I have no clue! Ask someone else." As for Krystal, making hot dog and hamburger buns at home had clearly never occurred to her, even in passing.

Bethel answered. "I've never seen one, but that doesn't mean much. You should look through older cookbooks, especially from the 1950s. Before that, people didn't eat many hotdogs and hamburgers were a lot less popular. Women still baked a lot in the fifties, so you might—*might*—be able to find a recipe in an older cookbook. By the sixties or seventies, most people would've bought buns at the grocery store. Start with Grannie B's old cookbooks, then keep asking around and looking through every old cookbook you can find. Some of the old folks out at the Bower's might be able to help you out. Libraries got rid of books that were old, worn out, or just not popular, so they probably won't have any cookbooks that old. The high school home ec teachers might have a few old ones, though, from when everyone had to take home economics classes. They didn't have much money to replace books in the last few decades."

Gisela looked animated. "Cookbooks? We have these, but they are too expensive for most people to buy one or have so few recipes no one is interested. I have wanted to see an up-time cookbook for months but never have time to go to the library to look for one. Do you have a cookbook here that I could see?"

Bethel's embarrassment was obvious. "Ahhhh, hmmm. Finding good ones may take a few minutes. Last summer, we packed away all the Clevengers' cookbooks since the family was left up-time. I promised to bring over a few cookbooks from my house and get some others from the attic, but it never happened. That box in the corner is full of their cookbooks. I'll warn you now, they are a bit odd. And specific. They have things like *The Zone Diet*, which was popular in the late nineties, but you may find a few decent recipes somewhere in there, if you're lucky. They have at least two with nothing but recipes for Christmas cookies. No good general cookbooks at all. I'll bring the ones I promised Krystal tomorrow. Next weekend at the latest."

Within minutes, Gisela was thoroughly engrossed. She asked lots of questions about what different cooking terms meant. After an hour, Bethel begged off answering any more questions because she wanted to walk home before sunset. Walking became more dangerous as it got darker and colder, and the sidewalks developed patchy ice. Gisela was still sitting in the dining room, cookbooks spread on the table in front of her, when everyone else went to bed.

When they came downstairs the next morning, she was still at the table, head cradled on her arm over a slightly damp page of the *Better Homes and Gardens New Cookbook* while she snored. Loudly. Being a dutiful younger brother, Dietrich woke her as soon as Anna Maria asked him to. He tapped her on the shoulder, his face an inch from hers when her eyes opened. Pulled out of a deep sleep, with Dietrich's weird expression *right there*, Gisela let out a startled *yip* and jerked backwards, falling off her chair and onto her butt on the floor before wiping the drool off her cheek and swatting her brother away, to the laughter of everyone else in the house.

Two Weeks Later

Bethel's head was barely visible over the large bundle she carried down from the attic. "Look what I found! Rag rugs! While I was searching for those old cookbooks, I moved a bunch of stuff around. I bet Grannie B and her sisters made some of these. Do you mind if I take a couple? We turned the thermostat down and the floors are cold on my tootsies in the morning."

Krystal nodded. "Take your pick. She's your grandma and I'm sure she'll be happy to know you want them, so sure. Are there more upstairs we can use here?"

Bethel nodded. "There's a whole stack of them in the front corner. All these years I thought that sheet covered an old coffee table! I also found the cookbooks I was looking for and a box of old records. I found a few that weren't damaged too much by the heat, but most are melted to some degree after being in a hot attic for years. If someone ever gets around to trying to save up-time music, perhaps they'll find a way to salvage those."

Krystal took the records. "We should bring the rest down to keep the damage from getting worse. I'll make space in the linen closet. Every blanket and most of the towels are in use now with so many people in the house, so there is space in there. Did you find any other treasures up there?"

"I think there may be some journals from Grannie B and Aunt Anna's mom, but they're in Italian so I don't know. Piles of old magazines. Why do people keep so many old magazines? There's a box with what I think were some gorgeous old sweaters from the fifties, the kind with beads sewn all over them, but mice got into that box in a big way. I wouldn't even try to rescue the beads. It's nasty. I didn't go digging any further than that. Oh, and this weird gadget. We need to ask Aunt Anna and Grannie B what in the world this thing is."

* * *

"Young lady." Only Irene Flannery called Anna Maria Schneider 'young lady.' "What is your lesson plan for this class on making rag rugs that I hear you are teaching?"

"The students bring scraps from home, and I show them how to make the rugs. It's pretty straightforward."

"You have children. How many ways do they find to mess up things you think are 'straightforward'? Adults are no better. You need an outline for the class, you need a material list, and you need a *plan*. Do you have a plan? No, I can see you do not. You are probably busy with your family this afternoon. Are you free tomorrow afternoon?" Anna Maria nodded, confused by Irene Flannery yet again. "Good. I will come over after lunch, at 1:30, and help you create a lesson plan. Have the table cleared and those books and papers I gave you handy, as well as the materials you need to make one rag rug."

"Um, okay, I guess. I will see you tomorrow at our house." Anna Maria walked away from Mrs. Flannery and toward her own family. "*Frau* Flannery has decided I need a lesson in teaching tomorrow afternoon so, fair warning, Irene Flannery will be in our house tomorrow afternoon."

"I have to stay after school." Agatha wasn't a fan of Irene Flannery.

"My boss said I need to stay late at work." Heinrich wasn't a fan either.

"I have baseball practice tomorrow." Dietrich wasn't afraid of getting kicked in the head by an angry horse or killed in battle. *Frau* Flannery was an entirely different matter. He firmly believed she could stop a Croat raider in his tracks with one of her blistering vitriolic attacks.

"I'm going to see if the bakery is hiring." Gisela didn't mind *Frau* Flannery, but she didn't want to be subjected to any of her lectures, either. Why the woman couldn't accept that drinking beer, especially small beer, at any age was *normal* was a mystery to her. The other up-timers seemed to understand. What was so magical about turning twenty-one? Avoiding her was easier.

Anna Maria raised an eyebrow, the pointed to them one at a time as she went through their excuses. "There is no school tomorrow. You are the boss. You didn't make the baseball team. And you can go to the bakery at any time to check for a job. But I know *Frau* Flannery, too, and accept all your excuses."

CHAPTER 5

Tina's voice was tired. "I know it's hard, Greg, but we need to accept reality and take the leap. I'm not happy about the situation either, but it's not exactly a secret that I'm sick. Even up-time with medicine, my weight made it hard to do a ton. Will you at least agree to talk to the young woman? It's freezing outside and she walked over here from the Refugee Center."

Greg was pissed, his tone accusatory. He didn't want strangers in the house, poking around. Helping refugees for a few weeks was one thing. Hiring them to live there indefinitely was another. "How did she know we—*you*—were thinking about hiring someone? Did you start advertising already? If so, you should have told me that 'we' had made a decision."

"No, I didn't. I mentioned thinking about hiring help in passing to Linda and Bethel last week, and Bethel said something about it to Krystal, and Krystal helps at the Refugee Center sometimes, so now we have a young woman on our literal doorstep. No advertising, no decisions without you, but she's here now and I'm too tired to argue with you."

Greg relented. He knew she was right. Seeing how sick she was left him frustrated and angry that he couldn't help her. Now here he was taking that anger out on her! Agreeing to hire a housekeeper was one thing he could do to help her, and he had to accept that as enough for today. "Fine. But no promises. I don't like the idea of servants like we've turned into modern robber barons or coal kings. We're normal people!"

Greg's complaint mirrored Tina's feelings, but she refused to let her emotions have control. Even before the Ring of Fire, she had health issues, they were just controllable then, or at least felt controllable. Tina was still a fully trained nurse and as soon as they knew what had happened, she understood what that meant for her. She was terminally ill with only a few years to live, and she had to ensure that her family, kids and husband, were in the best possible position when she left. She wasn't one of those fools who thought that meant finding a new spouse for her husband, but she was a hard-headed pragmatist. Now that they lived in the seventeenth century, "leaving them in the best possible position" meant convincing Greg to hire long-term live-in staff. Multiple live-in staff, in fact. Greg agreeing to start the process of hiring staff was a huge weight off her shoulders.

"Thanks. I'll bring her in from the mudroom. She should be warming up by now."

Slightly uncomfortable and unsure how to act around these new 'up-timers', Marge Beich dropped a small curtsy when she entered the room. "Thank you for talking to me."

Greg took the initial lead while Tina sank down into her favorite recliner. "Please, have a seat wherever you like. Tell us what you are looking for and how you came to be in Grantville."

Even more uncomfortable to be told to sit on such fine furniture, Marge sat on the edge of a straight-back chair, desperate not to dirty or damage anything. She would never earn enough money to fix even the tiniest scratch or stain on such expensive items. "I moved here from north of Jena. I have training in many things. I can iron, be a lady's maid, watch the children, cook a bit, and help with the garden and lands. I am willing to do many different tasks as part of a job. They did not tell me what kind of job you have to fill, so I don't know what you need."

Tina answered. "To be fair, that's because we don't know. We just started thinking about hiring someone. We weren't quite ready to start looking, but then Krystal sent you over and we decided to go ahead and talk with you. I'm sick, I'll die in the next few years," Marge took this with the aplomb most down-timers demonstrated when death was discussed, "and we need someone to help in the house and with the kids when I'm not well enough. We have two small children. Our daughter Christina starts kindergarten in the fall, so that will help, but little Jimmy is still in diapers and that can be a lot of work for me."

Greg had an important question. "How did you learn so many skills? Most down-timers I've met have a single job they learn and then try to master. How did you become such a jack of all trades?" Strictly speaking, that wasn't true, but most did stick to the same career path, so to speak. (Calling 'ladies' maid' or 'night soil collector' careers didn't sit well with most up-timers.)

Deciding she had better be honest, Marge answered. (Who knew if these up-timers had a way to detect if she was lying? It wasn't worth the risk.) "I have a hard time keeping a job. I get bored, then I ask questions, sometimes I suggest ways to change things to make life easier or things work better. Then my employer asks me to leave. It happens too many times to remember. I wanted to go to Latin School, university even, where I have heard they would not get so angry about the questions, but I am a girl. So, I stayed home and got these jobs. When I heard about Grantville, it sounded too good to be true. Then I lost another job, so I came here, hoping to find a job I don't lose so quickly."

"The unvarnished truth. I like it. How about you, Tina?"

"I do, as well. If we hire you, you will stay here with us, of course, but we don't have much spare space. Like I said, we haven't discussed the idea of help much yet, but if we hire you, your bed will probably be an air mattress on the floor in the kids' room at first. Are you okay with that?"

"Yes. What is 'air mattress'?"

Two Weeks Later

Greg could admit to her when he was wrong, one of the many things Tina loved about him. "I'll admit it: You were right, Tina. Having someone to help around the house has, well, helped. Marge is distractable, but the kids like her. Knowing that you can take a shower or bath without the kids screaming for you when I work late is a relief."

"I even get afternoon naps now, and I don't have to carry the laundry baskets up and down the steps. I can see why she has a hard time keeping a job, though. I swear she could be ADD. She's always getting distracted by things and trying to figure stuff out. You know that little trashcan full of dryer lint I'm always forgetting to empty into the trash? She took it, all of it, to make fire starters! I think she may be selling them, but I'm not sure, and I don't care. She doesn't have any interest in girly things, from what I've seen, but the way I've seen her looking at that busted up old toaster in the garage? Do not be surprised if she asks for tools to try fix it."

"Anything else, oh light and love of my life?"

"Only one thing. Didn't we toss a whole box of CDs we wanted to dump somewhere into the garage last winter? She has music on all day, and we don't have enough to choose from in the house. If I hear that *VeggieTales* CD one more time, I may lose my mind. I'm sure there is one more kid's CD in the box, possibly two. That will let her rotate it, at least, and hopefully she can find a few more she and the kids like. I mean, I *liked* that *VeggieTales* CD two weeks ago! But enough is enough."

With a courtly bow, Greg said, "Anything your heart desires. I shall away to the home of your mechanical beast to find this music thou requesteth of me, my fair lady love!" With a giggle, Tina watched her husband grab a blanket like a cape and stalk out of the room like an old-timey TV villain in search of his prey.

* * *

Gisela answered a knock at the door. Krystal had warned her that Aunt Bethel was bringing Aunt Anna over after church, but she didn't warn her Aunt Anna was ancient like Grannie B. Having expected someone closer to Aunt Bethel's age, Gisela reverted to automatic habits in her surprise, dropping a curtsy and saying, "Good afternoon, *Frau* Reed."

Anna gave her a withering look that would've done Irene Flannery proud. "I worked hard my whole life. I am not now, nor will I ever be, a person you curtsy to, and the name's Onofrio, not Reed. But no offense was intended, so none taken. I've seen the little cooking TV show you youngsters put on. Bethel tells me that you want to learn more up-time recipes. It just so happens that baking has always been my passion. Barb, Grannie B to this lot," gesturing around the room, "was only a passable at it, no matter what her grandkids tell you. That's why I took all of Mama's cookbooks and recipe cards, including the ones in Italian, when she got too sick to cook."

Bethel looked surprised and excited. "I didn't know Nonna Rosa ever wrote down her recipes. Can you translate them into English for me? Do you have her alfredo sauce recipe? How about her pasta machine? Please tell me her pasta machine didn't get lost or left behind!"

"Hmph. You're a lousy cook, Bethel, but I don't want the recipes lost and I'm an old woman." This tacit agreement to give Bethel the recipes was followed by some unintelligible muttering in Italian. From experience, her relatives knew it was about the 'younger generation' not speaking Italian or appreciating their heritage. "Have one of the youngsters help me and we'll translate them together. They might even pick up a few words in the process. Linda Bartolli speaks Italian, she can help if none of you lot will. Now for you, young lady. This" she waved a tattered old cookbook around in the air "was Mama's pride and joy. Barb tried to find this when Mama went to heaven, but I already had it. Barb waited too long." Anna was smug. "After we got off the boat from Italy and they finished processing us at Ellis Island, we went to Little Italy. Papa always said there weren't any jobs and Mama said the houses were too small, too dirty, and too close together. No gardens anywhere in New York City. So, we went to West Virginia to get Papa a job and Mama a garden. But before we left, she got this cookbook, second-hand. Her very first step to being an American, even if they did say all kinds of nasty things about us Italians and how we weren't 'really' Americans back then. I think it's just the thing to help you out, but never forget it's a loan." With that, she plunked *The Settlement Cookbook* in front of Gisela. The 1903 version. "Some American women wrote this book to help immigrants assimilate and become 'real' Americans."

Gisela brushed her hand across the cover. "Something written to help newcomers to America learn how to make American food and be more American? I can't wait to read it! I have been reading some of the 'cookbooks' in this house. There are so many!" She couldn't help being amazed at a life of such plenty that a regular family had a dozen different cookbooks with hundreds of recipes to choose from. And the ingredients! These cookbooks took owning expensive spices like cinnamon and cloves for granted. Apparently, average families could even afford to buy *figs*! "The only one I can understand everything in is *Yum! I Eat It!* I never heard of a cookbook for children before, but many of the words in the other cookbooks are hard to understand, like sauté, braise, and dice, and I understand all the word in this children's cookbook. Does dice mean to cut food into squares like dice? What does bread have to prove? It is bread! It has to rise, then bake, then get eaten."

Anna grinned but held in her laughter. "I wondered the same thing myself. Proving just means the bread has to rise, thereby 'proving' that the yeast is still good. Tell you what, we'll go through some of the recipes together. You show me the words that don't make sense, and I'll show you how to do them in the recipe. Then you will know the description in German. We could write a little booklet to help down-timers understand our up-time recipes and make a few bucks selling it!" Not entrepreneurial per se, Aunt Anna had shown a consistent knack for finding ways to make a few dollars here and there for her entire life.

Anna Maria entered the room in time to overhear this last comment. "I approve! Make the money, child! Your cooking club friends can be your guinea sows."

"Guinea pigs," Aunt Anna corrected absentmindedly. "I have decided. We will do it!" Gisela looked back and forth between the other two women, knowing the decision had been made for her.

"*Frau* Onofrio, the cooking club is having problems with some things that we cannot find. The hardest right now is no brown sugar, but at least we have baking soda and baking powder again. The up-timers were complaining *a lot* about not having it last fall, so the rest of us were relieved when the grocery stores started selling baking powder again and we stopped hearing the complaints." Gisela was at her most respectful with Aunt Anna.

"Humph. Young people. You all think everything should come from the store. We used to make both of those, back in my day. Mix molasses in with white sugar to make brown sugar. Mix cream of tartar and baking soda to make baking powder. You tell me when your next meeting is, and I'll come teach you young folks a trick or two."

"Before you dive into that, I have a non-cooking question for you, Aunt Anna. What is this?" Bethel gently laid an odd round gadget on the table in front of her aunt.

Anna's face lit up. "The sock knitter! That little gadget makes socks so much faster than knitting them by hand. When I was little, we didn't have these store-bought socks all you youngsters are used to. We had to knit our own, like the down-timers do. Hand-knit, a pair of socks took a week. With this little baby? An hour. I loved that thing when Papa brought it home. Not so much after a few years, but I sure did love our sock knitter when it was new."

Agatha tended to get stuck repairing the family socks. "Can you teach me how to use this?"

"I guess so. It's been a long time, and it needs some TLC before you can even think about knitting your first sock. Take care of that, then come talk to me. Now, if you'll all stop pestering me, I'd like to get back to baking with Gisela."

After Aunt Anna left, Bethel left out a sigh of relief and flopped into a chair. "That went better than I expected. She's no Irene

Flannery, but Aunt Anna can be testy. She likes you, Gisela. A lot. By this summer, we might get her on the TV show! That would be a hoot."

May 1632

"Gisela, have you looked at this *Settlement House Cookbook* Frau Onofrio gave you? I know you've paged through the recipes and even tried a few, but have you really read the book beyond that?"

"What are you talking about, *Mutti*? It's a book of recipes. What else is there to read?"

"Right here." Anna Maria plunked the open book down in front of her daughter and jabbed her finger at a heading. "Pages X-XI. 'Course of Instruction as given by The Settlement Cooking Classes'."

"Okay?"

"Why the questioning voice? Your Cooking Club! Every week, you do cooking classes. Every week, you are trying to figure out what to teach. Every week, I watch you scramble because no one planned enough. Worse yet, I must listen to *Frau* Flannery complain that I have not yet made you do all the class planning she is making me do, as if I don't already have enough to do. This book *has the classes planned for you!!!* There are twenty-four lessons, which is almost half of what you need for the entire year already planned! Two for every single month of the year! How are you *not* seeing this as a heaven-sent blessing? You can repeat them year after year, with some variations. Maybe the second year, for the nineteenth lesson, you show a new ice cream making machine or a different flavor beyond vanilla. Or you split the twenty-first lesson in half and have soup and scraped beef different weeks. Look at it!!!"

Gisela gave her mom a hard look, then started thumbing through the book, looking at the 'course of instruction' laid out in the book. As much as she hated to admit her mom was right, it was a solid plan, perfect for the TV show. The lessons would need moved around a bit, modified some to fit the seasons and so on. Overall, she didn't think many substantive changes would be needed. "I'll show this to the rest of the club. We were already talking about finding a cookbook to have reprinted to raise money. This almost certainly puts this cookbook over the top as the clear winner, but without the lesson plan reprinted. We need to hold something back so they keep watching the show! Reading the newspaper articles, too. We talked about making our own *Grantville Cooking Club* cookbook someday."

Anna Maria snorted. "That's a big dream, girlie. Your own cookbook! But if it can happen anywhere, it will happen in Grantville. What is the Club doing with the money from the newspaper, by the way?"

"Still working on it. Right now, it's in a bank account. There isn't enough to do much yet. We keep going around and around in circles about what we'll do, someday."

"Can you remember to talk to the others about the lesson plans in this book?"

"I'll try to remember to bring it up." Anna Maria knew that non-committal tone. Her daughter would *not* 'bring it up', even though she liked what she read. Anna Maria would do it herself or, if she was feeling cranky, she might sic *Frau* Flannery on them. Better yet, Effi

Schuetzin. The down-timers had insisted Effi "must be" part of The Cooking Club because of her demonstrated skill creating recipes at the Refugee Center, and because of how well known that had made her in Grantville. (They were right.) The biggest problem with involving Effi would be getting the cookbook back once she got a decent look at the thing. After considering the situation for a while, Anna Maria decided the easiest way was probably to point it out to *Frau* Onofrio and let her take it from there. The cookbook had belonged to her mom, after all.

* * *

Anna Maria was nervous. Ten women registered for her new class, a mix of up-timers and down-timers. There were even two on a 'waitlist' in case someone cancelled. She had only recently learned how to do the craft herself. Ever since Bethel found a stack of rugs Aunt Anna and Grannie B made during the Great Depression in the attic, Anna Maria fell in love with the simplicity of them. Every time she put her feet down on a rug when she woke in the morning instead of a cold, hard floor, she felt like a princess. The floors weren't even truly cold in a Grantville house!

Once they saw how taken she was by their old rag rugs, Aunt Anna and Grannie B both spent time making new ones with her while Mrs. Flannery helped her develop the class. She had written a supply list, step-by-step instructions, a short history of the craft, and a few small homework assignments, such as finding more scraps and sorting them by color to create new patterns. Every step and detail were neatly written in a precious up-time spiral notebook Mrs. Flannery insisted she use, with an even more precious up-time fountain pen she could refill from a bottle of ink. Hardly any of those had come through the Ring of Fire. She knew this craft would be popular with down-timers. The up-timer interest surprised her, though. She had assumed they all knew how to make rag rugs, but apparently not.

It was so simple, and yet such an elegant way to reuse old things if the rag man didn't come around much or didn't pay enough. Grantville didn't have regular rag men at all. She couldn't believe no one had thought of it before: braid together scraps into a long, long, looooonnnnggg braid. Roll the braid into a circle or oval. Sew the sections of braid together so they stay together. Put it on the floor. Have warm feet. Brilliance! Or put it on the wall, if you had a particularly drafty wall, the way rich people did with tapestries. Up-timers had never done it, but you could also make smaller, rectangular ones to cover windows. There were so many ways to use this craft they had forgotten or written off as a waste of time.

Since the sun was bright and the weather nearly perfect, even if the up-timers were bundled up in layers, the class was held outside. Following a short, calming prayer, Anna Maria walked outside. "Hello, ladies! Did you all bring a basket of rags and scraps? A needle and some thread? Grand! Let's get started on your new rag rugs! These are simplicity itself. We are going to braid the scraps, stitching ends together if you need to, then coiling them into a circle. The coil will be sewn together. Up-timers used these as 'throw rugs' on the floor, but I think they can also be hung on drafty walls or cover windows that need shutters. While we work, let us storm our brains for more ideas."

The weather really was lovely. When they left, each woman had braided and sewn together a long enough section to set a pot on, which was one of their ideas. The braided fabric would keep the food warm better than simply setting it on a table. Another suggestion was making a blanket.

Ilsa, a skinny, the less charitable might say bony, woman declared, "I will sit upon mine. The wagon seats are hard. Chairs are hard. Church pews are hard, although it is right for the church pews to be hard. But if I sit upon this, these things will not be so hard on my bottom."

Hearing this, the other women thought upon her suggestion for a minute. "I will sit upon mine as well." No one knew who spoke first, but they all decided that sitting upon these small rag rugs they had made was a grand idea. The new 'sit upons' would keep their skirts cleaner, and drier on wet days or even just when the dew hadn't evaporated yet. Within two weeks, Anna Maria had so many requests for the "sit-upon" class that she was teaching them every day, sometimes two a day. Part of what Mrs. Flannery was teaching her was how to teach other teachers, so she started training her first new assistant craft teachers to help meet demand.

By the time demand for sit-upon classes slowed, her business had received a nice boost, she had two teachers partially trained to help her, and their next craft class was ready to go: making grocery bags. There were two classes, one for net string bags and one for heavier fabric ones. With newcomers arriving in Grantville every day, Anna

Maria eventually had one teacher working nearly full-time teaching nothing but bag making and sit-upon classes, and Irene Flannery convinced her to take the real teacher training classes at the Vo-Tech to improve her teaching skills.

✳ ✳ ✳

As the wife of a well-known Grantville pharmacist, Bethel had point on the show today. "Hopefully most of you have tried potato chips by now, and possibly French fries, maybe even another kind of potatoes. We know how hesitant you all were to try them, but we didn't mislead you, did we? Potatoes really are surprisingly scrumptious! You can see for yourselves how easy to grow they are. When you don't have much money, or you need to hide your crops, potatoes are your friend.

"We have another food for you to try that you might be equally skeptical about. Oats. Stay with me here. Just because horses eat something doesn't mean people can't it too. We're going to show you two ways to enjoy oats. Oatmeal is basically oats boiled in water or milk with flavor added, like cinnamon and apple or raisins. Oatmeal was a *hugely* popular breakfast up-time, and it's super easy to carry with you when you travel. Just add water! The second recipe is granola, which can be eaten lots of ways and also travels well, especially as granola bars."

Liesl stepped up. "When the up-timers suggested eating oats, I'll admit it, I was appalled. Oats are animal food! I thought they were joking until I they showed me packages of 'oatmeal' and 'quick oats' that came through the Ring of Fire. One man showed me a cookbook full of nothing but oatmeal recipes, of all things. When I finally tried oatmeal, the taste wasn't as bad as I feared. I don't love the stuff, but I have had far worse while traveling. Granola, on the other hand, is tasty. It's crunchy with other things mixed in to improve the taste. Granola is a good topping for bland food.

"One quick announcement before we start. The Voice of America is going to start broadcasting our program! Please listen to WVOA for more details."

"Now, let's get cooking!"

June 1632

"Mama, I want to teach a class."

"Truly, Agatha? Why the sudden interest in teaching?"

"A friend cleaned the sock knitter and Aunt Anna taught me how to use it. This sock knitter will be such a massive time saver! I know a class will do well."

"How can you teach a class with only one sock knitter?"

"Oh, right. Didn't *Vatti* tell you? I thought you knew. *Frau* Onofrio used another kind of sock knitter, too. It doesn't do as nice a job, but the design is so simple she could draw it from memory. And did. *Vatti* made several for me. I'll use those for the classes so we can see if changes are needed. He found an experienced apprentice to work for him making more of them, and we'll sell those."

"What about the sock knitter from the attic?"

"Jerry Hart helped me find a guy who is trying to copy that one but he's super busy and has a lot of other things to do first."

"What if they can't do it?"

"After six months, the rights revert to me. They can't make any sock knitting machines in competition with me for five years."

"How much does Aunt Anna profit? Both sock knitters are her devices, and I'm guessing at least some of the advice as well."

"Aunt Anna said it was Grannie B's, and Grannie B said it was Aunt Anna's, then they both said it was their mom's, then they started arguing about who made better socks. In the end, they said neither of them ever wanted to see the stupid thing again and it was mine to keep. They even wrote it down to make it official."

"The undersigned, Anna Albana Onofrio and Barbara Albano Reed, do hereby relinquish all claims, monetary or otherwise, to the infernal contraption also known as a 'sock knitter' to Agatha Schulte, may she never regret the choice to take the detestable thing off our hands and possibly inflict it upon the rest of the world."

Anna Maria laughed. "Even that far in the future, old people never change. Just make sure no one knows they referred to it as 'infernal'. What are your plans for this? A class every now and then?"

"Oh no! *Herr* Hart told me that he overheard Mike Stearns telling someone that Greg Ferrara mentioned Doctor Nichols is worried about socks."

"Socks? Of all the things for a doctor to worry about? Socks!" Anna Maria shook her head in wonder at the craziness of up-timers. *Verrückt* indeed.

"I went to the Red Cross and asked them why he was so worried about socks. They sent me to a nurse, and I told her about the sock knitter. She sent me to Doctor Nichols. He spent nearly three minutes talking to me! He said that if people keep their feet clean, dry, and warm, they stay healthier. To do that, they need more pairs of socks, but socks take time to make, and people do not have the time to make enough socks. I could've told him that last part. He liked the machine a lot and said that once we fix it and start manufacturing them, assuming we find someone who can, I should tell the TV people that he said to do a TV 'informercial' about the sock knitter He made me repeat the word, then write it down. 'Infomercial.' They are supposed to reshow this 'informercial' a bunch of times because he really, really wants people to have socks."

While they were talking, Heinrich had walked in. "That was one complicated conversation. Can you go back and give me the short version?"

Agatha gave him a quick smile. "Sure thing! The up-timer doctor thinks people with extra socks have warm, dry feet and that helps them stay healthier, so he wants people to have more socks. He likes this little machine to make socks quickly. If we can re-create it, he vouched for us to get a TV spot to sell them. I'm going to teach a class to test how well the little one works, but I want to have the better one before we do the informercial."

"Dang. That's impressive, young lady. You might earn enough to have a good dowry for yourself. You must reconsider marketing the small sock knitter, though. It could bring in enough capital to fund developing the other one. Make sure to keep your *Mutti* and me involved. You are too young to run a business all by yourself. You need your family to keep an eye out for you."

✻ ✻ ✻

"Marge, it's not personal. You must know you're a lousy housekeeper, and you said yourself you don't like taking care of kids." Greg had been firm. Hiring Marge was Tina's idea, so she was stuck firing her.

Marge's tears threatened to spill over and roll down her cheeks. "I know. I wish I could argue with you, but I can't. I don't even want to. I hate cleaning houses." Tina held her tongue, wanting to point out that Marge never really *did* clean her house. "But at least I finally know what I want to do. Computers. I love them. But there are so few, and finding a job with them is so hard, perhaps I am wishing for what cannot be."

"Perhaps, but maybe you will get one of those jobs. Many people are afraid to even touch the computers we still have, much less try to operate one. I talked to Greg. We have a new nursemaid starting tomorrow so you can't stay in the children's room anymore and the house is full, but the weather is nice right now. There is a storage room under the carport. You can stay there for the summer, if you wish. That will give you a little time to find a new job and a new place to live."

"Thank you, *Frau* Ferrara. This is most generous of you. I am glad you have found a someone to help so the children don't bother the housekeeper. A lady like you should be able to rest, not work and

73

make yourself sicker like a commoner. Most can't afford to rest, but most know how important it is when you are sick." Since she was not working there anymore, Marge said something she normally wouldn't have. "Your *mutti* is right about that. You must rest more."

Tina's eyes narrowed and flashed at that. How much she rested was a sore point between her and her mom, but Marge meant well, so Tina let it drop. "You are welcome to visit and listen to music with me sometimes. Greg just doesn't appreciate gospel music. He barely tolerates Mom's organ music." Tina became pensive for a moment. "I wonder if Grantville could ever get its own actual, honest-to-God gospel choir. There weren't enough people before, but now?" She shrugged. "Maybe. Here and now, the problem is getting people who can sing gospel. Most people are too stiff to do a good job of it. Not in my lifetime, but hopefully someday!" The joke was definitely macabre.

August 1632

Mrs. Flannery sat down next to Anna Maria while they waited for mass to start. "You must sell your instructions to make these sit-upons of yours so people in other towns can make them as well. You cannot teach many in person, but you can sell many copies of the instructions. People can mail-order them for a few *pfennigs,* then make their own sit-upons, rag rugs, and whatever else they desire at home, wherever they are. I have seen women making them in the park while the children play. They send them to family and friends in other places. I peeked over the shoulder of one drawing a diagram of how to make one. Truly, teaching such a skill is not easy and you have the knack. She does not. I have seen the instructions you wrote for yourself to make sure you do not skip steps when you teach. You can sell this."

Seeing Anna Maria's confused expression, Mrs. Flannery patted her hand. "Mail order is a new way to do things, like teaching classes was. You'll get this too. I'm sure someone can help you, and I know there are people who can copy the instructions cheaply. You might want to learn knitting and crochet next. I have a few things I can give you." She stood up and moved to her normal seat in another pew, leaving Anna Maria pondering, yet again, what on earth had caused Irene Flannery to help her so much. She certainly wasn't known for being a kindly old lady!

One day, in the grocery store, Anna Maria had mentioned to a friend that Mrs. Flannery was generous and helpful to her. The up-timers in the store who were close enough to hear had turned to stare at her. One said, "I do not think those words mean what you think they mean," and then the other up-timers started laughing and continued about their business. But it was true. For some unfathomable reason, Irene Flannery enjoyed helping her. Even her advice to take teaching classes at the vo-tech had been helpful. Now this offer to give her even more things! She truly was generous, to Anna Maria.

Bethanne Kim

♪

CHAPTER 6

September 1632

"L ast year, kids and schoolteachers were the only ones who celebrated Halloween. I'm glad the teachers made sure they had a chance to dress up and to a little trick or treating in their classrooms. Mostly cookies and home-made treats." Aunt Anna had loved Halloween since she was a little girl. Getting dressed up was *fun!* "We should make Halloween treats for the show during October."

"Can you explain 'Halloween' please?" After more than a year, it was easy to forget what a different world Liesl and some of the others in the Cooking Club were born into.

"We celebrate Halloween, which you probably consider pagan and wouldn't ever celebrate, but that's a different matter. We do. It's the last night of October and the old wives' tale was that the souls of the dead came back to visit on Halloween night. You could leave a treat out for the spirits, or they would play a trick on you. Eventually, when people stopped believing that, kids started dressing up in costumes and 'trick or treating' for candy.

"They carry a plastic pumpkin, pillowcase, bag, or whatever. When they get to a door, they ring the doorbell, hold out the bag, and say 'trick or treat', then the person gives them a treat. Mostly candy bars but those are definitely gone. For October, I think our Club should focus on making candy bars and other treats, and not just on the show. We could have a party for all the kids in the park. You tell us what down-time baked treats kids would like, things that are easy to hold like cookies. Giving out things like pudding would require them to have a container to hold the pudding. We'll find recipes for up-time candy-bars and other treats. The kids can all dress up and get treats."

"We need to discuss this 'Halloween' a bit more. This sounds like something that will cause big trouble with the priests and people who already think Grantville is aligned with the Prince of Darkness. I don't know about everyone else here, but the idea of celebrating a night 'the souls of the dead come back' sounds like a bad idea." Most of the down-timers nodded vigorous agreement.

Aunt Anna deflated. "There must be something we can do. I love Halloween so much! Getting dressed up is fun." They were all silent for a minute. "If we have trick or treating in the afternoon and everyone is safely home by dark, would that help?"

The down-timers thought about this. Effi spoke first. "It would help, but I still don't know about it. What are these costumes? Are they devils and evil things, or are they angels and saints, or something else entirely?"

"Ah, well, that depends on what the kids like. Everyone has a different outfit. Some are train engineers, fire fighters, and other jobs they want when they grow up. Some dress up in old-timey clothing or princess gowns. Clothing styles their parents wore when they were in high school are always popular. There were some who dressed up in costumes, up-time, that we wouldn't want them to wear now, down-time.

"How about this, I can call Lyle Kindred. We'll work with him and run a special series of articles on Halloween and how it's family fun. We'll include things that can't be done, like dressing up like a devil. Or," with a significant glance at the other up-timers, "Jason Vorhees. Never mind about Jason. I know, some will never be convinced it's not evil, but I'm not willing to give up one of my favorite fun holidays just because some boobies are being poopy-heads!" That got the desired laugh.

"You know what would be fun? Making something with that new tabasco sauce I heard Reva and Ikey are selling, and maybe some of their habaneros. 'Devilishly hot food!'" As a child, Aunt Anna had once taken a big bite out of a habanero pepper. She had never forgiven peppers for her trauma.

Krystal loved her grand aunt, but she wasn't about to let her spoil peppers for everyone. "You're so bad, Aunt Anna! You know if we even hint at something like that no one will ever eat those peppers." The whole family knew Anna hated peppers with a fanaticism most reserved for the arch-rival of their favorite sports team. "Stop grinning like that! I'll tell Harry Lynch on you if I hear another peep about it. That's right. We know who you have a crush on, and I saw the way he cradled those two bottles of tabasco he managed to snag at the supermarket."

"Point. Set. Match. You win, girl. I'll behave. But you hush your mouth about Harry Lynch. I'm no schoolgirl for you to be gossiping about." *And I can see the way Harry looks at Betty Ruth Snodgrass, skin and bones that she is. Hmmm. Maybe I should bake him something? Betty Ruth failed home ec back in the day. Who fails home ec?* "While we are talking spicy, have you been using the spice bush at all? They grow wild in the woods, and there's a massive one out behind the house Irene Flannery grew up in."

"Way to change the subject Aunt Anna, but I don't know about spice bushes. Can you do a show on them?" Anna nodded. "Great!"

October 1632

"Anna Maria. I'm helping Sam box up more stuff from Mrs. Flannery's house and move it into her garage. His garage now, I guess. He's trying to clear out one side to move his car over there. Anyhow, we found a box labeled with your name and a card enclosed." Krystal was more than a little curious about what was in the card, but she could see the box had crafting supplies. When she agreed to help Sam clear out a room in the house he had recently inherited from Irene Flannery, Krystal didn't expect the place to have so much stuff packed into it.

Anna Maria read the letter slowly, then a second time, and a third, glancing frequently at the bright colors in the box. "Mrs. Flannery says she wants, wanted, me to have her grandma's knitting needles and all the knitting and embroidery supplies she had in her house. There should be some books in there." She was quiet again, before reaching out to caress the rainbow of yarn. "The colors look like I could wash them over and over and they would never fade. The white is so white, the black is so black, and this yarn that has so many colors all together in the same skein! This is truly amazing. I have never seen anything like this rainbow yarn."

Krystal removed the books and looked at them while Anna Maria went through everything else. A few minutes later, Krystal glanced up from a pattern book to see Anna Maria in shock, holding double handfuls of metallic and brightly colored embroidery floss to her chest, tears leaking down her cheeks. Krystal put her arm around the older woman and gave her a friendly squeeze. Anna Maria smiled weakly at her. "I never expected to be rich enough to own such bright colors, even in embroidery thread. This is not a fortune, but it is a fortune to our family. We will be able to afford a shop after we sell this yarn and thread. Maybe not in Grantville, but a shop where I can teach these crafts Mrs. Flannery loved. I will keep the books to teach what is in them."

Halloween 1632

"Having trick-or-treating in the town park was an inspired idea, if I do say so myself. And I do." Anna Onofrio had never been afraid to toot her own horn. Old age and hearing loss hadn't changed that a whit. "This is what we did when I was a girl. With no cars, the houses felt so far apart! By the time we finished, we were too tuckered for school the next day. So, the parents decided to simplify life and have one event in town, at the park. Like this but with fewer angel costumes." Looking around for a minute. "What is with all the angel costumes? And the old-fashioned outfits?"

Marge had met Tina and her family and their friends so she could experience an up-time style Halloween. None of the up-timers seemed to understand why so many kids were dressed like angels, so she answered. "It's the churches. If the kids are dressed like angels, saints, or part of the nativity (not Jesus, of course), it's harder to say they are being pushed to do the devil's will, so most of the parents decided to be safe. Saints are popular for the Catholics. Those are the 'old-fashioned' outfits. I've seen a lot of Wise Men wandering around, too. The Calvinist kids came out with friends and are wearing masks, so their parents can pretend they didn't participate. A lot of them are knights in armor with their faces covered. Most of the ones not dressed as saints, angels, knights, or wise men are up-timers, adopted by up-timers, or Old Grantville Hands who don't care what the church thinks since they don't ever plan to move anywhere that doesn't have religious freedom again."

"Huh. Good thinking, that. Especially the Calvinists. Those articles in *The Grantville Times* seem to have helped people understand and accept Halloween better. The kids were excited! The pastors, priests, and all those guys did a good job, too." Bethel didn't love Halloween quite as much as Aunt Anna, but few people did. "I'm glad we've revived it, even if things are being tweaked a bit. This is the first Halloween I haven't seen a single kid as a sheet-covered ghost, and there's not a 'Jason Vorhees' costume in sight, either. Those are classic last-minute, I-forgot-my-costume costumes."

Tina was sitting in a camp chair, watching the kids. "Yeah, it's a bit surreal. In some ways, it's a normal Halloween with the kids running around and getting treats. In others? The Ring of Fire blew away our old normal. Between the newspaper articles, the literal sermons at all the churches and on the Voice of America, and people having conversations, most people got the message that costumes better not give any impression of devil worship or smack of evil. Almost reminds me more of kids getting ready for a Christmas pageant than Halloween with all those angels and wise men. Lots of shepherds too. I think shepherds may be the down-time I-forgot-a-costume costume. But still, I couldn't have imagined slips of paper with Bible verses as a Halloween treat!"

Raymond had taken a rare afternoon off to spend time with Linda. "The honeyed small beer is popular, but the kids don't exactly look excited about those Bible verses, kind of like up-time non-caramel apples, but they don't look as bummed as I would've expected. Even the up-time kids accept it. They aren't the down-time equivalent of toothbrushes. Which, now that I look around, someone is handing out. There is a line to get the new down-time toothbrushes. I never, ever, in a million billion years, thought I would see a line to get toothbrushes at trick or treating.

"Too bad more of their parents didn't get into the spirit and dress up. Fingers crossed for next year!" Raymond was one of the few who loved Halloween as much as Aunt Anna. Everyone had agreed trick or treating was better done during the late afternoon than after dark to save on lighting, and to further decrease any possible association with The Dark Side. "I'm pretty stoked to fit into this old Han Solo costume from college. Never expected it to fit again!" He swelled out his chest. "And Bethel kept telling me to donate it. But here I am! If only she would wear the Leia bikini...."

Bethel swatted him over the head. "Stop pouting. You think I should wear that in public? In 1632? You're crazy. Outside, in this weather, in any year? You're double crazy. I promised to wear a Star Wars costume and I did. Be happy with that." Greg snickered at her answer. He couldn't help himself. Raymond had been snookered. When Bethel agreed to a Star Wars costume, Raymond was *definitely* thinking Princess Leia, not Chewbacca.

Tina eyed her costume enviously. "I wish I had thought of that. You are *warm!* With all the weight I've lost," over sixty pounds, "I had so much fun choosing from all kinds of cute costumes I couldn't wear before, but I am *cold* and very jealous of your warm costume right now. The jacket Greg brought for me helps, but my legs are practically ice cubes. It's worth it, just this once, but we are for sure going home soon and skipping the after-party at St. Mary's!"

Bethel sounded faux-scandalized. "Hush your mouth! It's not an after-party! It's a Special Bible Lesson. With treats. The Cooking Club really outdid themselves with those homemade candy bars. Maybe some music. But not a Halloween party! What *would* the priests think of such a thing?" She fluttered her open palm in front of her forehead in mock distress, like a Southern belle in an old movie.

CHAPTER 7

November 1632

"Wow! It's amazing how many members we have now! When the Cooking Club started a year ago, it was just a few parents getting together. Look at us now! We've half-filled the Gardens all by ourselves. I think everyone knows why we are here, but the short version is that we have a steady income from the newspaper articles and the radio shows, and the cookbook reprint is coming out any day now. That money is accumulating in a bank account, doing nothing. What do we want to do with it? Thoughts?" As founding members, Gisela, Bethel, and Liesl were leading the proceeding.

"Could we buy a kitchen? Or build one? Having a test kitchen or a place to meet outside of people's homes would be fun. Maybe we could even start taping the show there."

"Are there any stoves or up-time kitchen gear we can buy for the club?"

"How about investing in a farm?"

"Could we buy a clubhouse?" That one got a groan, mostly from up-timers.

"Are there any cooking schools? We could create a scholarship."

"What businesses could we invest in? There must be some small businesses making kitchen gadgets we can help out."

When the brainstorming finally petered out, the discussion started.

"There may be some stoves we could buy, but probably not. There are always kitchen gadgets around, so we might be able to buy some of those."

At the end, Liesl summarized the comments. "A 'cooking school' would be interesting, but no one here knows of one and we don't have enough money to start our own. Stoves are hard to find, but we'll all look for one, and we'll keep an eye out for kitchen and food companies we can invest in. Since we expect an income bump when the cookbook is released, especially in the first month or so, we'll talk about what to do with any club funds more after Christmas. Enjoy your walk home, everyone! We are adjourned."

❋ ❋ ❋

Sarah Jane Rogers had joined the Cooking Club almost as soon as it started but she wasn't a regular attendee. She had managed to duck being on the TV show for nearly a year, but her luck had run out. Her day job working for the newly formed Grantville University Press had run smack dab into her social time with the Cooking Club when the club decided to reprint *The Settlement Cook Book of 1903.*

Shepherding the cookbook through the printing process was now literally her job. No other version had come through, but everyone agreed they should include the year because down-timers knew older up-time things translated better to their life needs. Now, she was on the show both as a presenter and to promote the cookbook. She said a small prayer and took a steadying breath as the producer counted down to "on air".

"Hello, everyone! You all know that our TV show here relies a lot on information in *The Settlement Cook Book of 1903*. Over the past six months or so, we have been working with Grantville University Press, which is my regular job, to translate the book into German, test the recipes to make sure they work, find substitutes for things that aren't available in the here-and-now, and generally ensure everything is ready to print. The first run will be coming off the presses in January!

"We pushed so hard to get the book out so you could buy copies for Christmas gifts, but there simply wasn't enough time to finish all the work. We still think *The Settlement Cook Book of 1903* could be the best Christmas gift for the cook in your life, so we are offering a special Christmas deal! If you pre-pay for a copy of the book, you will receive a suitable-for-framing copy of the book cover to present at Christmas, and the book will be available for pick-up or shipped, if you aren't near Grantville, as soon as they are printed." That was Sarah Jane's idea, and she was proud that her bosses had run with it. "We aren't setting any limits on the number of pre-orders, but this will be the only time we offer a copy of the book cover like this."

Effi took over. "And now, Sarah Jane and I will show you all a true up-time holiday tradition. You tried French fries and loved 'em. Then you got some potato chips. Next up: mashed potatoes! Simple, but filling, and oh so yummy, or so the up-timers all assure me. I'm still not as comfortable as they are with eating these" she caught the producer's expression before she said something bad about potatoes "'root vegetables' they love so much. Mashed potatoes are so much a part of up-time traditions for both Thanksgiving and Christmas that up-timers assure me that imagining either holiday without 'mashed taters', as many call them, just feels wrong.

"Now, let's get cooking!"

December 1632

Krystal woke up and was drawn downstairs by the tantalizing aroma of fresh gingerbread and pine. Heinrich was decorating with fresh evergreen branches while Gisela baked gingerbread. "The gingerbread and apples look so lovely on the evergreen." Seeing her surprise, Heinrich explained more. "This is how we decorate. With the cookies and apples on evergreen branches, and small Christmas Angels around the house. Since you didn't have these things last year, we are helping decorate this year, but we are leaving spaces for the tree, socks, and other important decorations."

The small wooden Christmas Angels were new to Krystal, and she was sure they would be new to most of the other up-timers, too. "They are so cute! You need to make more. You could sell a ton!"

"I was hoping you would say that. This is what I have been working on when I am not at my job these last months. I did not see them in up-time homes or shops last year. We made them in my home in the Ore Mountains. When I became a journeyman in Augsburg, I showed some of the other carpenters how to make them to earn spending money. I am a master now, although I have no shop, and these are well made. I have found a journeyman to work for me. If we sell enough, perhaps at least one of us can 'quit our day job' and focus on woodworking."

"You have a new journeyman? That's fantastic! Have you found a spot for a shop?"

Nervous, Heinrich blurted his answer. "Mayhap. I must talk with you. The shed in the backyard. I wish to empty and rent it." With all the new people and businesses, finding a shop to rent in Grantville was a coup for any business.

"That's tiny! How will you fit everything in there?" Krystal had questions.

"At first, it will only be the two of us, and what Ty and I are making is tiny. When we need more room, we will have to move. But in this space, we can leave tools and pieces out at night without having to worry that a child will accidentally harm themselves or what we are making. A small building is also easier to lock up tight to keep things safe from thieves." So far, she hadn't said no, which was a relief for Heinrich.

"Don't you need electricity for the band saw and stuff? We only have electric for the house and garage, not the shed."

"If we had an entire band, we would need a bigger space, but we have enough space for the hand tools we need. As I said, it will only be two of us and most of what we use are small hand tools to make small angels. We will pay you fair rent. Also, my journeyman wishes to sleep there. He will provide extra security."

Grannie B and Grandpa Eli still used the rent from the house to pay their bills, so there was no way Krystal would say no or offer to let them use the space for free, but she had to be sure. "Let's walk out and look." Once she was satisfied the space could be emptied and two adults could work in it, she and Heinrich agreed on rent and shook hands. "Congratulations on your new shop, Master Schulte!" His surprise was clear. "What, you hadn't quite realized you are opening your own shop again?"

Krystal couldn't resist teasing him for a few minutes before getting serious again. "When you start to outgrow this space or if you want a storefront for the holidays, you might consider using the garage, but your mystery journeyman can't stay in the shed. Winter nights get too cold. If you want to use the garage as a shop, you can continue to store finished items in the shed, so you have more space to work, or the other way around. Turn the shed into a small shop, do your woodworking in the garage. Just something to think about."

Hearing her say Ty couldn't stay in the shop threw Heinrich for a loop. Ty needed a place to live. After living with them for over two years, Krystal refusing to house Ty hadn't even occurred to Heinrich. Perhaps it was her being in denial that the all up-timers were going to stay in seventeenth century Germany causing problems again, just when Krystal's family and friends, including the Schultes, were starting to believe she had accepted her new reality. "Please, *fräulein*. Could you reconsider letting him stay in the shop? Housing is a standard part of the 'pay' for apprentices and journeymen. If he can't stay there, he will not agree to work for me. Finding and training someone new before Christmas will be difficult." *More likely impossible.* He was literally standing in front of her, hat in hand, twisting the poor old hat out of what little shape remained.

Krystal was startled by that. "Huh? I don't mean turn him out! We need to find a space in the house for him, that's all. If he can build a wall in the bathroom, he can have half that space as a room, then he'll be warm and cozy all winter and I won't be worrying we'll wake up to find a frozen corpse in the shed some morning, not to mention what my great-grandparents would say if they found out he was sleeping on the floor in an uninsulated shed!" When her great-grandparents bought the old farmhouse, they modernized the old homestead by turning a first-floor bedroom into a new, then-modern bathroom with indoor plumbing. It was enormous for a bathroom, by any standard. Turning half the space into a separate small room would leave the bathroom normal-size, and faster to heat. Bonus!

Deeply relieved, Heinrich drew a breath and asked what he hadn't been sure he could. "If you truly mean this, then we will have a small store in the garage over Christmas. Anna Maria and Agatha would like to have their classes in there, if you approve, and we can sell things made by the whole family. This will be a test for everything we have been doing."

"Great! I'll get Sam to move his car to his own garage. I'd move mine too, but it's still up on blocks, so that's too much work for just a few weeks. If things go well and you want to keep using the garage, who knows? I might even decide to sell my car." Heinrich was secretly thrilled to hear her say that. For a year and a half, she had kept that car in the garage, of no use to anyone, because she couldn't accept that they were never going back to their old life. This was a huge step in the direction of admitting she was never going to drive again.

* * *

"We are doing something a bit different this week. Instead of cooking food to eat, we are cooking, baking, really, Christmas decorations! We have one down-time recipe, gingerbread, and one up-time recipe, salt dough. Both can be formed and baked, but gingerbread is usually made into thinner, more delicate shapes while salt dough is given to five-year-old kids to make ornaments. Up-timers make the dough into flat disks that parents press their infants' hands into for keepsakes. If that isn't enough decorating for you, for the rest of this month, we will be showcasing some up-time decorating traditions in addition to cooking." Effi was one of the most popular hosts of the show. Every few months, they had a special segment where people asked her to use an unusual ingredient and she obliged. Every now and then, the Grange asked her to use something they wanted people to eat more of, like potatoes and oats.

While not as popular as Effi, Linda was a frequent presenter on the show for the simple reason that her house was often empty, so she had time. "We have received more than a few letters complaining that following along at home is harder since our viewers don't know the ingredients in advance. We spoke to Lyle Kindred at *The Grantville Times* and Wayne Eberly at The Dollar Store. Starting next week, *The*

Grantville Times will publish a shopping list three days before our show and The Dollar Store will have a special display of everything you may need to make the recipes.

"Finally, if you want something to give someone something extra-special for Christmas this year and have deep pockets, the Cooking Club has four, count 'em *four*, original up-time boxes of banana bread we are auctioning off in something called a 'silent auction'. You can place bids on them at the library where one box can be seen on display. Before anyone gets any ideas, we removed the mix from inside so it's nothing but the empty box on display. The proceeds will be used to buy equipment and other cooking supplies for the Cooking Club and TV Show. When you are bidding, please remember this: those up-time bananas don't exist anywhere in the world right now and may never exist in this world. These may be the dodo bird of cooking! About to go extinct and exist no more.

"Now, let's get cooking!"

* * *

Using what she had learned the last Christmas, Anna Maria Schneider had a brisk, if small, business selling advent and ribbon wreaths at the fledgling Grantville Kristkindlmarkt, barely worthy of the name, and out of the garage. By the second week of Advent, she was teaching classes in making up-time-style ribbon wreaths in addition to classes on Advent wreaths. By the end of the Christmas season, she had earned a healthy profit and had a group of women ready to learn more up-time-style crafts. As she started teaching her first assistant how to be a teacher, she appreciated more and more why *Frau* Flannery had pushed her to take the teach-the-teacher classes as soon as she could. Teaching someone else how to teach was an entirely different kettle of fish from understanding how to be the teacher herself.

On top of all that, and Agatha's sock-weaving classes after school and on weekends, Anna Maria was planning aa few classes to teach down-time crafts to up-timers. The first would be weaving fabric tape for all the myriad normal household tasks the narrow strips were used for. Since her students needed tape looms, Heinrich added those to his little store. He created a special line of Grantville fabric looms featuring the silhouette of famous buildings such as the high school and the library along the top edge. The Dollar Store, among others, continued doing a brisk business selling Heinrich's looms long after Anna Maria ran out of customers for a regular tape-weaving class.

Anna Maria and Agatha both enthusiastically accepted donations of up-time crafting supplies as payment, especially copies of books and patterns. Handwritten was fine, as long as Anna Maria was allowed to look at the original to ensure everything was copied correctly and that she could understand the directions. One poorly copied set of ultimately unusable instructions guaranteed she didn't skip that step again. In the long term, those patterns would be invaluable for Anna Maria's intended business.

Unfortunately for Agatha, manufacturing the sock-weaving machines was slow going. Her first goal had been to get into the Wishbook, but that didn't happen. Then she wanted to sell them for

Christmas, but she missed that deadline too. Businesses in Grantville were busy and finding good help was hard. Flush with enthusiasm, she was certain that her goal of finding a business partner, not just help, would ensure she could find someone. It did not. The up-timers knew it was good product but didn't understand why socks were a big deal. The smiths she needed to work with were men and didn't understand why the sock knitter was a big deal. The end result was that the fancy sock knitter wasn't bringing in any money for her dowry yet.

As part of her teacher training, originally intended for elementary school teachers, Anna Maria had to teach in an elementary classroom. Once she finished the training, she would have a fallback job as a teacher if she ever needed it, which was nice.

✳ ✳ ✳

Everyone was gathering their things to leave but Father Mazzare wasn't quite done. "Hold on folks, you can't get out just yet. There might be a few people in town who haven't heard yet! Julie Sims Mackay, mother-to-be that she is, has apparently had some conversations with the North Pole and arranged for Santa Claus to make his very first visit to Grantville in our new German home. He will be doing a meet-and-greet at the high school on Christmas Eve.

"As you might imagine, Santa has a big job and he needs some help, especially for the small ones. Julie is helping him by collecting presents for the children, which can be left in several different places, including St. Mary's, and asking for volunteers to take them to the high school in time for the party."

The men's Bible study class had already been told Julie Mackay needed a Santa Claus and warned not to talk about it where children might hear. Then they were told who and what a "Santa Claus" is, along with a physical description of him and his suit. Surprisingly to the up-timers, the flying reindeer and magical gift bag weren't the sticking points. The big one was Santa going down the chimney. In summer? Sure. In summer, plenty of fires were banked overnight and, with a bit of shimmying, he could manage it. But in late December? No. Utterly unbelievable that he could pop in and out of everyone's chimneys like that and never catch on fire. And the red suit was ridiculous. A nice dark gray or green, even dark brown, would blend in and help him remain undetected. A red and white suit would make that almost impossible.

"Finally, *Herr* Schulte has some Christmas Angels for sale after the service, and a portion of the proceeds will go to help the needy. Go in peace, serve the Lord!" Gisela and Anna Maria had both insisted on this to get free publicity for Heinrich's new business.

"Thanks be to God!" For the millionth time, Father Larry wondered how many of them were thanking God that the service was over and they could leave. "Almost all of them" was certainly a low estimate.

Gisela was unusually quiet on the walk home. Krystal finally nudged her with her elbow. "Penny for your thoughts."

"They are not so interesting. I thought I saw General Pappenheim in Grantville yesterday, but mistakenly thinking you saw a famous person is not interesting. I saw him when we lived in Bohemia and it looked like the same person, but we are not in Bohemia now, so I could not have seen General Pappenheim. Also, I am trying to think of a thing I can do to help those orphans and Julie Mackay. I am not so good with crafts and things, like *Mutti und Vatti*, but I want to help."

"If you could give them anything in the world, what would it be? Answer fast!" Krystal gestured for Gisela to answer fast.

"Gingerbread cookies. I would make them gingerbread cookies like I made in Bohemia. My cousins were bakers and I helped in their shop, but the gingerbread guild wouldn't let me become a member, not even an official apprentice. I loved the smell and the way the dough felt when I mixed it. I was better than one or two of the journeymen. Not as good as the masters, but more than good enough to be a journeyman, if I wasn't female. But there you have it. Guild rules. No women. Plus, I would need expensive spices my family does not have enough of."

Krystal glanced around to make sure no one else could overhear. "I may have been holding out a bit on you. I still have almost all the spices that were sent back with us in the house since they aren't really ours, but they're starting to go stale, so I guess it's okay to use them now. It is for the children, after all. There is a giant container of cinnamon and full or nearly full regular size containers of nutmeg, cloves, and some other spices." Krystal was startled by Gisela's squeal of glee and giant hug.

"There is no guild here to stop me and you have the spices! I can make them gingerbread cookies! If we have the sugar, I may frost

97

them, just a little. They will be so excited by this treat!" In her excitement, Gisela skipped a few steps, then twirled around, before continuing more sedately.

When they got home, Grannie B sent Sam into the kitchen for a box in the cabinet over the fridge. "Since the arthritis in my hands started getting bad, these beauties have just been packed away. Gisela, I have seen how much you like baking and I heard you talking about making gingerbread cookies for the orphans. Eli's the one going deaf, not me!" Everyone rolled their eyes at that. They were both going deaf, Grandpa Eli was just getting there faster than Grannie B. "As we came back here from St. Mary's, it occurred to me that these might be fun for you to use while you're living here, and that most likely no one had looked in those hard-to-reach cabinets over the refrigerator." Grannie B and Grandpa Eli had lived in the house for more than fifty years before moving into the Bower's Assisted Living Facility and renting out their home to help pay for it.

Gisela took the box Grannie B held out for her and peaked inside, unsure what she would find. Grannie B explained. "They're cookie cutters. I bought the oldest ones when I was a young bride and wanted to impress my new husband with my baking. I kept adding more over the years, a few here and there, until I ended up with the collection you see there. I know my sister said I can't bake, but she was just being ornery."

"And snooty, Grannie B."

"And snooty, Krystal. I bake well enough. Not all of us aspire to be Julia Child."

Gisela was at a loss for words. "There are so many! They are so simple, just outlines. I can make many wonderful things with them. I...I don't know what to say. I will make beautiful cookies for the children with them, and also bring some for everyone at your new home to enjoy. They are so different from the ones we use for gingerbread. The ones we use are carved wood, which take much time and skill to create, then we press the dough into them. Few people have more than one or two, if they have any. I will treasure being able to make so many different things with your simple cookie cutters, and to decorate them any way I please." As she spoke, Gisela was sorting the cookie cutters into two piles.

For a moment, the down-timers were afraid the up-timers had been insulted, but Grannie B smiled. "That would be the wonderful, thank you! But you go have fun with them. You might even teach Krys and Sam a thing or two about baking. Maybe use them on that cooking show you kids do! Now, tell me what those two piles you are making are about."

"These, I understand what they are." Gisela pointed to the larger pile, full of stars, trees, and circles. "These, I do not."

"Ah. Easy-peasy." Grannie B picked them up one at a time and explained the cookie cutters. "Santa Claus. Also Santa Claus. I'll just make a little pile of Santa Clauses. Reindeer. Sleighs. Gingerbread men, and women. Dreidel. Snowflakes."

"Wait. Go back. Dreidel? What is dreidel? Also, that doesn't look like a snowflake. They are little dots or flakes. Not pointy like that." Anna Maria was enjoying seeing the new treasure her daughter got to play with laid out.

"Technically a Hannukah thing, not Christmas, but it's close enough. Jewish kids played the dreidel game for Hannukah. A few years back, the schools decided learning about other cultures was important and since Hannukah and the dreidel game were part of that whole effort, our kids learned the dreidel game and I got the cookie cutter. We have the actual dreidel game tucked away somewhere in one of these boxes of Christmas decorations, if any of your kids want to try it."

After nearly a year and a half, the Schultes all thought they were immune to being shocked by the casual, deep-seated, bred-into-the-bone religious tolerance of the up-timers, but every now and then something happened that shocked them all over again. Seeing a Jewish symbol casually mixed in with Christmas things was one of those shocks, magnified by how matter of fact the up-timers were about it. It wasn't that they didn't care that down-timers might be upset. They weren't ignoring the issue. They weren't even doing anything deliberate to get a reaction. Any of those the Schultes, and other down-timers, could have understood. They might not have agreed, but they could have understood.

The mere idea that having a Jewish game, or a cookie cutter of that game, mixed in with Christmas things could be a problem, an *actual* problem, a thing that mattered more than spilling a glass of water in the sink mattered, was so utterly, completely, and incomprehensibly foreign to the up-timers that they simply could not process it. They simply couldn't grasp that it was a problem. Anna Maria knew that no matter how she tried to show them or explain it to them, the up-timers would eventually reach a point where they *accepted* that mixing Jewish traditions in with Christian traditions was a problem, but never a point where they would truly *understand* why there was a problem.

It was kind of like explaining to a down-timer why it was okay for a woman to walk down the street in a swimsuit or shorts and a t-shirt. They might eventually agree that it was acceptable, but many would never, in their bones, believe that a respectable woman would do such a thing. They could only reconcile the fact that respectable up-time women and girls did such things by putting them in a different box, just like the nobility, because everyone knew that nobility followed rules that were a little bit different, and so did the up-timers. *Verrückt.*

"Sure?" Gisela's answer to Grannie B's offer to teach them how to play the dreidel game was definitely a question, addressed to her parents.

Heinrich answered. "Perhaps another day, *Frau* Reed. Today was already busy. I am seeing Sam pulling on his boots, so I believe it is time for you to head home. The bus back to the Bower's must be leaving soon. We will look in the boxes for these dreidels that are shaped like the cookie cutter. Perhaps we shall find them and you can teach the us."

Grannie B started wrapping up in her coat, scarf, and all her other winter gear. "Well, if you can't find 'em, they're easy enough to make. Let me know either way. Hey, you could start carving some and sell them in your store!"

"I'm busy carving angels right now, but I'll keep your suggestion in mind for next year." *'In mind' perhaps, but not in my shop. No need agitating people when my shop is brand-new. Although, we could make them and have another shop sell them. The Dollar Store always needs small things. It would be a bit less profit, but we could perhaps build some relationships that way. Hmmm. Worth considering.*

✳ ✳ ✳

Gisela was too excited to wait to use the cookies cutters. Besides, the party was in a few days. The up-timers all said Santa Claus was for little kids, but everyone, not just little kids, was excited to see this famous up-timer for the first time, whether they admitted it or not. The next morning, Gisela had her mother and sister both out of bed early, baking batches of gingerbread so they would all be ready for the party. "We will make two dozen from every cookie cutter." Her mother and sister blanched at the prospect of so much baking.

"It is too many!" protested her mother. "They don't need so many."

"Tilly's Army is gone. No one is trying to kill us right now. We have enough food. Grantville is safe and they are having a party, so we will do this." With a merry, pleading look, "Please *Mutti*! The family I work for has gone to Magdeburg for the next two weeks, so I have time. The town has done so much for us. Julie Mackay has kept us safe. Agatha was *in the high school* when the Croats attacked and Julie Mackay fought them off! We must help her in this." They agreed on half a dozen of each cookie cutter. They would make another half dozen of each IF they had the time and ingredients, and IF Julie Mackay needed them.

102

When Krystal got home from nursing school, she was stunned to see food containers and tins stacked everywhere in the kitchen, more than a third of them already full. Even old popcorn tins were pressed into use. "What on earth? Why do you need so many containers? How many cookies do you plan on making?"

"Hi, Krystal!" Agatha was upbeat. "We are almost done cleaning up from the baking today. Mama said we will try 'chicken salad sandwiches' for dinner. Gisela insists we must bake hundreds of cookies, enough so all the *kinder* can have two at the party."

Krystal's eyes got wide. "Hundreds? In this kitchen? In two days?" She whistled at their nods. "Have you thought about asking to use the parish hall kitchen at St. Mary's? It will go a lot faster and I'm sure Father Larry will let you, if it's available. If not, one of the other churches may let you use their kitchen since it's for the party."

Gisela slowly nodded, considering the idea and deciding it had merit, but Agatha was the one who answered. "I will run over right now and ask!"

As Agatha started getting her coat, Krystal held out a hand to stop her. "Just call the church office and ask." Five minutes later, approval was received.

As Krystal made everyone chicken salad sandwiches for dinner, she watched Gisela gathering tools and supplies to use the next day. It gave her an idea. "Have you ever seen a gingerbread house?" They all shook their heads no. "Hang on a minute, you're gonna love this." When she came back into the room, Krystal put a boxed gingerbread house kit into Gisela's hands. "Kids love these. You make the house out of gingerbread, hold the pieces together with frosting, then decorate the outside with candy. Keeping the walls stable is always a challenge, but even when they fall apart, making gingerbread houses is fun!" Most people don't realize when they meet their one true love, but that was the moment Gisela met hers: gingerbread houses.

"And eating them! That's fun too," Sam chimed in as he walked through the kitchen, grabbing cookies as he walked by. "We made those with Cub Scouts. We got awards for 'used most candy', 'used most frosting', 'tallest', and all kinds of silly things. But the most fun was eating them."

Seeing her hesitance to open (and thereby destroy) the precious up-time package, Krystal grabbed it back and opened the package herself. "I know this is from up-time, but it's food! I can't imagine it's good to eat anymore. Look, a mouse already started chewing on a corner of the box. You should build and decorate it!" Laying out all the parts, she motioned to Gisela to get started. "Bring the finished gingerbread house to the party and they can use it as a decoration, then let people eat it while they are doing the clean-up. Bonus snack for the cleaning crew!"

Gisela was an artist at heart, and her medium of choice was baking. The night before the party, she used all the techniques she knew to make the small house perfect. As she was putting the finishing touches on the path to the door, Krystal startled her. "Did you stay up all night working on that? It's beautiful, but you look like crap. How did you make all those decorations?" Taking in the small tools surrounding the gingerbread house, "You did that all by hand?!? Wait here! I have something I bought Grannie B for her birthday before they moved, but her arthritis got bad and she never used it. You definitely should."

Gisela wearily started cleaning up, her energy deserting her now that the gingerbread house was built and decorated. Anna Maria came in, looked at her, and simply said "sit" before taking over the rest of the clean-up. "You were up all night, yes?" A heavy nod. "You go to bed. Agatha and I will wake you for lunch."

"Soon, *Mutti*. Krystal wants to give me something."

Krystal bounded back into the room. "Here it is! The 'Cake Master 100-Piece Cake Decorating Set' and *you're gonna love it*!"

* * *

Englishman and tool Justin Marbury leered at Gisela as he walked up, munching on one cookie and waving another around. "I understand you made these. I haven't seen one since I was little. Might be fun to play again. Who gave you the idea to make cookies shaped like a teetotum? I will see if they have a teetotum I can buy."

Confused, Gisela looked to Krystal for help. She knew Justin from nursing classes, before he quit supposedly to return to England. Too bad he had stayed in Grantville another year. "First of all, jerk-face, her eyes are higher up. Second, never heard of a 'teetotum.' That's a dreidel for Ha...," she caught Gisela's expression, "The holiday season."

Justin proceeded to explain, in painful detail, how the game 'teetotum' was played and how the pieces were designed. Then he explained how his grandparents had played it, and even 'Good

Queen Bess' had been a fan. In fact, according to him, *every* Englishman loved this 'teetotum' game, which was superior to anything created outside of England. When they finally escaped from Justin, Krystal and Gisela found Morris Roth, and Morris Roth made a quick sketch of the dreidels and found the closest down-time Jew he knew, Balthasar Abrabanel. "Do you know this game?"

"Teetotum? I've seen it in my travels. But what is written on the game piece? It's not the usual English letters, N, T, H, and P. Hebrew? I've never seen a teetotum piece with Hebrew letters."

"No, it's not. It's a dreidel, the Hannukah game, with Hebrew letters, not English. *The* Hannukah game. Every child plays the dreidel game." As Morris talked, trying to elicit some agreement or understanding, Balthasar kept shaking his head, clearly indicating he had no clue what Morris was talking about.

"Maybe up-time, but I've never heard of a 'dreidel' game. That," pointing at the outline, "is for playing teetotum. Come to think of it, I saw a German version with S, G, H, and N. Same game, though. Looking at the Hebrew letters, they could mean the same things: Nothing, Take all, Half, and Put in. But why would children play a gambling game for Hannukah?"

"I always wondered that myself, Balthasar, but the dreidel has the first letters in 'Neis Gadol Hayah Sham,' referencing the great miracle of the defeat of the Syrian army and the re-dedication of the Temple in the story of Hanukkah." Balthazar would understand the reference. The explanation was for the gentiles with them.

"I like it. Never heard of it, but I like the idea. Can I keep that sketch, so I don't forget about it with everything going on, Morris?

I'm going to share the idea. If we don't use Hebrew, the dreidel can be a small, easily hidden thing for our brothers and sisters living in areas that are not as…accommodating as West Virginia."

"Of course." Morris shook his head in sadness. Hidden Jews always needed things they could hide in plain sight. "The story always felt convoluted, but an English gambling game? I can't believe that's how the dreidel game started. I mean, I believe it because you are telling me, but at the same time, I can't believe it. I am not looking forward to telling Judith about this. I think the dreidel game may have been her favorite Hannukah tradition."

Bethanne Kim

PART 3: 1633

CHAPTER 8

January 1633

"It's so frustrating, *Vatti!*" Agatha wailed.

To her silent fury, Heinrich simply shrugged. "This is part of business, girl. If you want to be in business, sometimes you will fail. Sometimes people won't pay what they owe you, things will break that you can't afford to fix, workers will quit or run away. Sometimes another business is too busy to make the things you need. If you can't adapt, you won't stay in business. You still own the original sock-knitting machine, and you have profits from the small one. Now, you decide. Do you stay partners and keep waiting for him to figure out the problems or do you end the partnership and find someone else to work with? The biggest question is the simplest: do you think he can do it? Can he figure out the problem and start manufacturing these in large enough numbers to be a real business? How long has he already been working on it and how much progress has he made?"

Agatha's shoulders sagged. She didn't want to admit failure. She stayed silent.

Heinrich saw the realization she didn't want to say out loud. "Do you want me to talk to him for you?" Agatha nodded. "Well, I'm sorry, but I won't. You started it; you need to end it." She looked even more miserable after hearing that from her father. "I will help you. I just won't do it for you." That cheered her up, a little.

"Thanks, *Vatti*, that means a lot. I was so excited when we started! I could see all the women and families the sock knitter would help, how much time those machines could free up. Now it won't happen. All that work, and it didn't make any difference."

"Are you giving up so easily? Why aren't you looking for a different smith to make them for you? Did you even try to get in the line for tooling at Marcantonio's or Ollie Reardon's?" Agatha shook her head no to her father's questions. "You should try that new place. Braun and Scharff, I think. They can probably help you sooner, and they may know an experienced smith who can work with you to build a viable business this time."

Agatha sniffled into the new handkerchief her *mutti* had given her for Christmas. "Okay. But do I have to tell Gisela? She will never let me forget my business failed."

"Did it? It seems to me that you have two businesses. One has hit a rough spot, but your simple sock knitters are still selling like hotcakes. There are at least three different knock-off brands. If she still teases you, then I suggest that *you* never let *her* forget that you had a business while she was still playing with her gingerbread houses." Finally, he saw a faint smile grace his youngest daughter's face.

* * *

"*How much?*" No one could tell whose exclamation that was in the shocked hubbub.

Liesl gave the number again. "And that's for each box. Frankly, I was hoping for enough to buy a stove, maybe a refrigerator too, if we were lucky. I don't know who bought these, but we have a serious decision ahead of us. What do we do with this windfall?"

Everyone in the Cooking Club was stunned. "Can we think about it for a few weeks?" Linda had certainly never expected their little cooking club to turn into a mini empire when they started less than eighteen months earlier. A TV show, newspaper syndication, a radio show, a book, and now this. The amount of money raised by the little last-minute silent auction they had arranged before Christmas for four boxes of up-time banana bread was, well, bananas.

Liesl made a quick note to herself. "With a unanimous vote, the decision on how to spend the money we raised has been tabled until a later meeting. Next up, deciding our meals for February. The up-timers suggested 'chili' and that Alyse Ballentine be invited to the show since she is a gen-u-ine Texan, which is apparently important for chili. Linda, can you tell us a bit more about this chili?"

"For starters, it's a nice, thick, hearty winter meal. Chili fills and warms you from the inside out. Most chili has beef, but only a small amount. It's mostly beans and tomato sauce." Linda scanned the reactions around the room. "Oh my God, what is it this time? And yes, I know, blasphemy, but what is the problem with chili? We've made beef meals on the show before, and we had tomato sauce when

Aunt Anna was on last summer, so what is the problem with *beans* of all things?"

One quiet woman known to be a cook for some niederadel with pretensions spoke. "They are common. Simple. Vulgar, even. Such things are only eaten when one has no other choice." She shuddered a bit. "There are no armies reducing us to eating oats, beans, acorns, and all those other last-resort foods. We have options now." Her face was set in stone.

Linda thought for a minute before replying. This wasn't the first time down-timers had some reason to not eat something that made no sense to the up-timers, potatoes being the most noteworthy example. "We 're not trying to convince anyone to eat chili, or beans, as part of your regular diet, but can you agree that some people still eat beans because they are poor?" Grudging nod. "And that there might be a time, in the future, when more people will need to eat beans because there are few other options?" Another grudging nod. "Chili is a way to make beans, and tough beef, things you only eat when you have no other choice, taste better."

The cook still seemed suspicious but nodded her acceptance. "But no more beans! Not like the way you keep sneaking potato recipes in all the time. You have even been adding oats to recipes, like we're some kind of animals." She sniffed. "It's almost enough to make me quit this club."

As she left the meeting, Linda muttered to herself. "Willie Ray Hudson better appreciate what I'm doing here. 'Help the Grange', he said. 'Just mention a few foods now and then,' he said. 'It'll be easy,' he said. Ha! Easy my behind. Why can't the man at least give me something they haven't heard of instead of something they already know and hate?"

February 1633

Bethel stopped by the pharmacy on her way to the train station. "Raymond, I'm taking the train to Magdeburg for the weekend. I've never been, I'm bored, and I want to visit."

"Sorry, honey, I'm busy. This weekend doesn't work."

"I know. You're busy. Like always. I don't expect you to come, and I'm not waiting for a time when you're not busy. I'll find someone else to hang out with while I'm there. I'm sure you'll be fine without me." She paused, then gave him a perfunctory peck on the cheek before heading over to the train station.

Raymond's partner John Moss was standing nearby and overheard the whole conversation. After Bethel left, he cleared his throat, obviously wanting to say something. Raymond said, "Go on, spit it out."

"Dude, that was bad."

"What are you talking about? Bethel's going to Magdeburg for some sightseeing. She knows I'm busy working. No big deal."

"No, that was bad. I've been working with you for nearly two years, and I saw you two together in town for years before the Ring of Fire. She barely touched you. That was bad."

Raymond was getting irritated. "Why do you keep saying 'that was bad' like my marriage is in trouble or my wife is about to run off?" John kept staring at him. "What?"

"*That was bad.* She didn't ask if you wanted to go. She didn't invite you. She didn't try to schedule a time you could go. She literally said she is not waiting for you. And tomorrow is Valentine's Day, which you appear to have entirely forgotten. Two years ago, you called her every night at dinner time and apologized when you couldn't get home. When's the last time you did that? One year ago, you were both talking about all the cities and famous sites you wanted to see together. She just said you haven't been to Magdeburg. Have you even gone to Jena together? Erfurt? Have you gone outside the Ring Wall, for God's sake? When was the last time you had an evening together, just the two of you?"

Raymond looked like he had been slapped, which he had been, verbally. "Christ. You're right. That *was* bad. You're right. I'm an ass. Now I have to figure out how to fix it. If I can fix it."

"If you leave *now*, you can catch the train. Bethel left you an opening, *if* you want to catch her, and I'm pretty sure she wants you to catch her. She definitely wants you to *want* to catch her. Bethel Ann and I can cover the pharmacy. You've trained us well. Seriously, you haven't taken a day off since the Ring of Fire, have you? Take the whole week. You two deserve a little vacation. I'll tell your daughter." As John spoke, Raymond was pulling on his boots, grabbing his wallet, gloves, coat, and everything else he had brought with him that morning.

On his way out, he grabbed toiletries including a toothbrush and toothpaste, and stationary to write a love letter to Bethel on the train, or at least a solid apology for being a putz. "Put it on my tab!"

* * *

"I'm so, so sorry, Bethel. I've been so busy trying to re-invent up-time pharmaceuticals and learning about down-time remedies and how to integrate everything into a new kind of pharmacy that I lost sight of everything else. John said he can handle the place for a week. If you can get off work, we can have a proper vacation. Just the two of us."

Tears in her eyes, Bethel flung her arms around her husband and held him so tight his arms started falling asleep before she let go. "Thank you. I love you so much, but it's hard to love a person who isn't there, literally in your case. You are gone before I wake up and don't come home until after I'm asleep. There are more days I don't see you than ones I do. If I didn't see your laundry in the basket, I could forget we still live in the same house. I didn't tell you before I left, but I already took the whole week off. I wasn't sure if I would want to come home at the end of the weekend, or if you would even notice if I didn't. I mean, it doesn't really feel like we still live together." Hearing that, Raymond's heart sank like a rock. John was right. This was *really, really* bad. "I want to look for a house here." Seeing him turn ashen, Bethel realized how that sounded. "No! I don't want to leave you. I want to fix things. We own our house and the pharmacy. I want to take some of that equity and invest in land here in Magdeburg, but I wanted to check prices and see what is available before discussing it with you. I know you don't have much time. My friends like the idea. I chatted with Judith Roth about it at the Christmas party and she agrees. Two of my friends in the

Cooking Club asked me to tell them if I find a good realtor. They're considering moving here."

In some ways, this made Raymond feel better, but hearing all the other people who already knew, people who had time to talk to his wife when he didn't, made him realize how very little time he had made for her over the last two years.

"Oh, God, honey, what did I say?" The last time she saw him cry was at his mother's funeral back in '97.

"I almost lost you. For what? The first year, yeah, I needed to work a lot, but I still should've been home more. This year, Halloween might have been the only time I took off just to be with you. I honestly can't remember, and I'm so sorry. Between them, John and Bethel Ann can handle the business now. I can't quit being a pharmacist, but I can change jobs. They wanted me to work at Leahy when it opened but there was no one else for our pharmacy. I will talk to them when we get home and see if they still have a job for me. I'll make sure I'm still there when you wake up every day. I can't make promises about when I'll get home. I'll try, but at least I can be there in the morning." He suddenly brightened up. "Now that Brent is about to graduate and Bethel Ann has a job of her own, maybe I can turn his room into an office so I can spend more time in the house with you."

Now Bethel was crying, gentle tears rolling down her cheeks. "That would be wonderful. Amazing, in fact. The best Valentine's Day gift you could've given me. Yes, I know you forgot, but it's the first time you forgot. And the last time." Raymond made a mental note to make sure it really was the last time he *ever* forgot Valentine's

Day, and also to make sure they had a fabulous lunch somewhere with a great view the next afternoon.

April 1633

Gisela and her best friend, Margaretha Kniess, founding members of the Grantville Cooking Club, were in the kitchen, baking. As usual. More specifically, they were experimenting to find a way to hold the pieces of a gingerbread house together without using expensive frosting the way up-timers had. Gisela was determined to master the craft before Christmas, or at least get good enough to sell a few. Everyone else in her family seemed to be starting businesses. She didn't want left behind.

Gisela was getting annoyed. "If I didn't want to keep them eatable, making the buildings would be so much easier. Oatmeal dries nice and hard, but there is zero chance anyone will eat dried oatmeal on gingerbread cookies. I still don't understand why up-timers like the stuff so much."

"So? Make them decorative and not eatable. Make eatable ones later and charge more for them. Can your father and brother make us some real gingerbread molds?" Orphaned and left penniless as a teen, Margaretha saw a solid business opportunity for her friend, if she would just *grab it* instead of endlessly worrying over stupid details like how oatmeal would taste with gingerbread. If the woodworkers in Gisela's family could make patterns for the walls, roof, and other parts, it would speed the process up a lot. Speeding up Gisela's process could mean a business by Christmas 1633, not a few sales here and there. And, if she was very, very lucky, Margaretha might be employed by said business and start to save some money for a small dowry of her own.

"Hmmm? I suppose so. I can ask him after I figure out how to hold the houses together. What do you think about decorating them? Colored icing would be 'nifty', but plain white is easier."

"White is also cheaper. I think you are too much an artist and too little a businessperson." Margaretha felt strongly on this point. Gisela was careful with her money, she simply didn't focus on things that needed to be done to run a business, like getting gingerbread molds to make the process easier and faster. She could work on details like how to decorate them while someone else carved the molds. As a girl, Margaretha had helped her Papa run his store after her mother died from plague. "If Dietrich, or your father or anyone who can do it, makes you molds, then you can have fancy windows and doors and whatever else you like. All you need to do is trace over the outlines with frosting. If you make them beautiful enough, perhaps people won't be eating them so they can be held together with up-time cement for all that matters!"

Margaretha's frustration was getting the better of her, so she went outside to clear her head and calm down before she said something she would regret. Yanking weeds out of the herb garden allowed her to channel her frustration and accomplish some work at the same time. While she was out there, she took a few extra minutes to plant some seeds and enjoy the lovely day.

As she walked back inside, her entire focus on not dropping the remaining seeds in her hands, the delicate paper envelope being worse for wear, she bumped into Heinrich's journeyman, Tyrone, and knocked them both into the berry bushes next to the porch, spilling all the seeds in the process. "Oh…nuts!"

Tyrone looked and sounded perplexed. "Those are seeds, not nuts. I mean, I guess nuts are a kind of seeds, but they look like regular seeds. You know, seeds…."

Margaretha had mercy on him. "I just planted some vegetables and those were seeds I didn't use. I have been trying to not swear so much. I had a soldier tell me I was swearing too much, so I decided to make a real effort to stop. So, nuts!"

Tyrone laughed at that. "Let me help you gather the seeds-not-nuts you spilled, *Fraulein* Margaretha."

"Thank you. Out of curiosity, how did you end up named Tyrone? I've met lots of Hans, Johans, Georgs, and any number of other names, but never another Tyrone. It sounds up-time."

Tyrone blushed clear to his hairline. "It is. My name was Hans Bauer before I came to Grantville. Do you know how many Hans' there are? Too many to count, that's how many. All day long, I would hear people yelling for 'Hans' and have to look to see if they meant me. My whole life it was like that, but so much more here with so many more people. I was not even the only Hans Bauer! Shortly after arriving in Grantville, I saw a movie starring 'Tyrone Power'. My family is from the Tyrol and that sounds like such a strong name, plus Power sounds like Bauer, so it's not too far off. After a few days of thinking to be sure, I decided. I declared my name was now Tyrone Powers and stopped answering to Hans."

"So, you changed it? Like that?" Margaretha snapped her fingers.

"Yep."

"No one cared?"

Margaretha heard the grin in Tyrone's voice as he answered. "Nope. I had apprenticeship papers for 'Hans Bauer', but I went to the Guild offices in Erfurt and they gave me something to show that 'Hans Bauer' has changed his name to 'Tyrone Powers'. They didn't give me much trouble since they have problems all the time with papers when someone has a ridiculously common name, like Hans Bauer. My Journeyman papers all say Tyrone Powers, so they will be hard for someone else to use."

"I think that's the coolest thing I've heard all month. I can bring you some gingerbread from the next batch, if you want and Gisela says it's okay." By the time Margaretha turned around, Tyrone was back in the shed where he worked with Heinrich, and where she couldn't see his silly grin or the even sillier little happy dance he did.

May 1633

"We are agreed, then? The Grantville Cooking Club is going to use our money to buy a piece of land to build on. The bank has agreed that we have enough income from our shows and other ventures to ensure we can pay a mortgage, so we aren't limited to what we can pay for outright. Now, what do we want to use the building for, other than meetings? That will determine what and where we build, which will determine how much we need to borrow."

The discussion raged for hours. Ironically, the Cooking Club ordered dinner delivered so they could keep discussing. Several members had to leave to arrange for childcare or to let their families know they would be home late. Finally, they wound down.

"Please, let us all agree one last time, for the vote. The Grantville Cooking Club agrees that we will buy a piece of land within the ring wall of the Ring of Fire, if possible. If not, then within West Virginia County. The land will be used to build a cooking school. We will have enough land to grow a variety of fruits, vegetables, herbs, berries, and other foods we need, excluding grains which we will purchase, and to add outbuildings for things like butchering, a greenhouse, and other necessities as we are able. All in favor, say aye. All opposed, say nay. It's unanimous. Once we have the land, we will need to finalize exactly what kind of cooking school and who we want to teach but for now, we are adjourned. Go home!"

* * *

"*Vatti*, how can I do this? No one takes me seriously. Even when you come along, as soon as they find out I want them to make a machine to knit socks, they tell me it's a waste of time. Even when I show them the small ones and how many classes I have, they are amused. They don't take it seriously. They don't take *me* seriously. Why? Everyone knows about the Barbies! Why don't they think other young people can run a business?"

Heinrich had been expecting this. "You have a great product. You have a solid plan. You aren't the only one. Tons of people in Grantville have great products. A lot of them have a solid plan. Some even have both. You need to make them want to invest in you and your product."

Agatha practically wailed. "I've already talked to every blacksmith in Grantville and most of the ones within a half day walk! And the machine shops. Every last one says they are too busy already."

"Then find someone else to ask and find a way to show them you can sell a lot, like by doing that informercial and selling a ton of the small sock knitters."

Now she was getting mad at her dad. "There's no one else to ask! I've already asked all the masters at their shops! I told you that."

"What about the ones who aren't masters yet? Or visiting masters who don't have a shop here? Are there other smiths who could make this other than blacksmiths?"

Agatha sat thinking so long Heinrich fell asleep in the warmth of the sun. "A tinsmith."

He startled awake. "What? A tinsmith? What about a tinsmith?"

"A tinsmith might be able to make the sock knitter. The up-timers always go for the blacksmiths, but they don't seem to remember whitesmiths exist, so they aren't as busy. A tinsmith might be the answer. I will do the informercial, but I will also try to find tinsmith who can make them instead. I'm sorry, *Vatti*, but I think they will be better in metal. Thank you!" She gave him a peck on the check and ran off, presumably, but not necessarily, in search of a tinsmith.

I'm glad she finally figured that out. Wood really isn't strong enough, long-term, for the sock knitters. Heinrich pulled his hat down over his face and went back to napping.

* * *

"I don't know what to do with myself, Greg. John and I signed the paperwork saying he is now a fully trained pharmacist, and I own the land and building outright in exchange for training him. Bethel Ann is managing my half of the business. Now that it's done and I'm not working at the pharmacy anymore, everyone has told me that I have a month off before Leahy will let me start working." Without work and with the kids grown, Raymond was lost.

Greg stared down at his hands, twisting his wedding ring. "Mind a little free advice?" Raymond motioned to continue. "Go somewhere with your wife. You are both healthy, your kids are grown, and there are so many places we could only dream of seeing Before. Do you know I got to hold a Gutenberg Bible? In my bare hands? Without wearing those funny white gloves museum people wore? Crazy. Go. Take Bethel and visit somewhere. Find a Gutenberg Bible and hold it. Visit with DaVinci. Have Rubens paint her picture. I guess Rubens may have to wait, but I'm sure there are plenty of other once-and-future famous artists who are currently starving. Find one. Castles and hunting lodges like Versailles are all over the place. I bet there's at least one lordling or trumped-up merchant out there who owes you for saving someone in his family with your up-time medical knowledge. Call in the favor and go for a visit, all-expenses paid."

"I'll think about it. Going somewhere that expensive could send the wrong message, now that I'm a government employee."

"Stop making excuses. People *expect* that of anyone as prominent as you are, and you know you are. You have certainly helped people who own hunting lodges and feel they owe you. If you can't think of one, don't pretend you can't afford a nice trip. What, exactly, have you spent your money on these last two years? You haven't gone anywhere. Your mortgage stayed up-time. Neither of you buys much other than food. Just pick someplace within a few days ride and *go*. You have no idea what I would give for Tina to be well enough for us to travel. Everyone says there will be passenger planes going to Italy soon. That would be amazing!" Greg's eyes were glistening, a tiny bit. "Ask Bethel where she wants to go and take her there. Your kids are both grown now, so you could take a second honeymoon."

"I have been thinking of visiting the medical college in Jena to see their botanical gardens."

"No! Are you listening to me? You will be so busy when you start the new job. Spend the time *with your wife,* not working! My wife is dying and too sick to go anywhere. Yours isn't!"

Raymond was taken aback by Greg's vehemence. "You're right. I guess I've seen enough people in the pharmacy, and enough people who stopped coming in when we ran out of their medicine, to know that God never promises us another day, let alone a whole year. Bethel certainly made it clear that I haven't been paying enough attention to her. Thanks. I'm sorry for stopping by unannounced. I'll let you get back to work."

* * *

The carriage swung to a stop and a servant opened the door for Raymond and Bethel. Since they had kept the windows covered in a vain attempt to reduce the dirt and bugs inside the carriage, they hadn't seen the place as they rode toward it. Bethel spoke first. "It's a castle. An honest-to-God castle. Raymond, why are we at a castle?"

"Thomas Nehring told me it was a hunting lodge. I swear! When he was visiting Grantville, his daughter had a bad cut and I helped keep it from getting infected. Her condition was touch and go for a while. He was sure she would lose her foot, but she recovered completely. This is his way of repaying me. One month in his hunting lodge."

"Hmmm. He may regret his generosity. Our up-timer ways may corrupt his 'staff'."

A man who seemed to be the butler overheard. "If I might speak, your ladyship."

"The name is Bethel, and I am no ladyship."

He smiled. "Indeed. My name is Werner Wiegand, and I am what I believe you call a butler. In the last few years, the former owner of this estate invested rather more than he should have in rather the wrong things, such as microwaves and, before that, alchemy. *Herr* Nehring lent him rather more money than he could repay, and now *Herr* Nehring owns this hunting lodge. We have spoken about your visit, and I believe that he invited you here for a month *hoping* your up-timer ways would, ah, 'corrupt' the staff. In particular, your mania for kitchen hygiene. If you will follow me, your bags are already being taken upstairs."

* * *

Bethel Little poked at her breakfast, moving things around on the plate like a child trying to hide how little they were eating, even tossing a few scraps to a dog under the table. "Once it sank in that we were never going back, I knew I'd miss some things, like toilet paper and soda. The toilet paper issue has been sorted out and all the fresh bread makes up for not having soda, but every now and then something hits me. Do you know what I miss now?"

"No, my dearest, what do you miss now?" After more than twenty years of marriage, Raymond didn't make the mistake of guessing.

"A bagel with cream cheese. A solid, freshly toasted–or straight out of the oven!–bagel with cream cheese oozing out of it, washed down with a fresh cup of coffee or juice. Maybe a blueberry bagel instead of plain. After this long, I don't care. I'd even eat an anything bagel! There was this little café in Morgantown that made bagel sandwiches. Turkey with cream cheese. The last fall before we came here, I had a turkey sandwich with cranberry brie instead of cream cheese. Heavenly!"

Bethel's eyes were slightly unfocused as she remembered the pleasure of a warm bagel with oozing brie, the tartness of the cranberries the perfect contrast to the cheese and turkey, the firm bagel the perfect platform for the sandwich. Seeing her remembered pleasure made Raymond want to share in it, to have a bagel right here and now, especially since he didn't find their current breakfast any more appetizing than she did. Unlike some treats that were made from chemicals and extruded from machines, bagels were undeniably made from real ingredients in kitchens in small stores, at least in big cities like New York. In Grantville, they had been forced to make do with refrigerated mass-market grocery store bagels.

The more he thought about it, the more Raymond wanted cream cheese, too. Down-time had cows, so cream cheese should be doable as well. He hoped. This was so far out of his comfort zone, it was in a different galaxy, not just a different neighborhood. A fresh bagel with cream cheese, if he could figure out how to make them, would make a perfect "milestone birthday" gift for Bethel's fortieth birthday in October. The tough part would be finding the recipes. No way, no how did he have enough time for that.

The sound of a chair being pushed back roused him from his reverie. "Werner mentioned that we should visit the kitchen and there is no time like the present. Well before lunch." When they entered the kitchen, they watched the cook pushing scraps from their breakfast plates into a large stew pot hanging over the fire. "What are you doing?"

"Waste not, want not," Judith, the cook, answered.

"Well, yeah, but that doesn't mean you feed scraps to people."

The cook shrugged. "It was good meat. You only pushed it around. You wasted it. I won't."

Raymond and Bethel exchanged glances. Knowing his strengths, and weakness, Raymond prepared to retire to the yard and let this fight to Bethel. "Go get 'em, tiger. I'm going to look around outside while you start on this. I'll be back by lunchtime." As Raymond strolled outside, he saw a small boy weeding the garden and a slightly larger one cleaning tack from the stable. Since he was killing time while Bethel got to work making the kitchen hygienic, Raymond started talking to the boys. Cleaning tack and weeding were both chores it was easy to do while talking.

"What's your name, young man?" He addressed the one cleaning tack first.

"I'm Julius. That is my brother Samuel. He doesn't hear well, so he doesn't talk much."

"I see." Raymond walked a few steps closer and tapped Samuel on the shoulder to say good morning before Julius could stop him. When he turned, Raymond couldn't keep the surprise from his face.

Everything about Julius screamed panic at that. "Don't hurt him! He works hard. He doesn't get into trouble, not much anyway. He goes to church with everyone else. Please just let him work the way he knows how to. Cook doesn't mind the way he is."

Raymond held up his hands in a calming gesture. "Don't worry, I won't hurt him. I understand. He has Down's Syndrome. You say he has hearing loss?" An exceedingly tense Julius nodded. "That's normal. I'm glad you found jobs for him that he can do. Has he ever gone to school?"

"People like him don't go to school."

"Hmm. I'd like to talk to your parents. He could go to school in Grantville. His education would have been better up-time, but at least we can see about getting him some education so he can have a job."

"People like him don't have jobs, either. Not ones that pay. We don't have parents. Mine died when the Croat's attacked our village a few years ago. Pastor Gregory came through our town right after and I left with him. He already had Samuel. His family died before mine did, so we adopted each other. *Herr* Nehring is a good man, even if he does have a bad cook, so when Pastor Gregory learned he was willing to let us both live here, we moved here last year. People would take me, but no one else would take Samuel in because of the way he is. Living here, he has been weeding, sweeping, and doing other small tasks ever since."

Raymond wasn't too worried, but he needed to be sure. "What do you mean by a 'bad' cook? Does she hurt you? Is the cook a bad person?"

Julius' confusion was clear. "You had breakfast. I saw your plates. Do you usually not eat breakfast? One meal is enough for most to know she is a bad cook. No one here hurts us. This is a safe place for us."

Raymond looked rueful. "Ah, yes, we did notice she was not exactly the most skilled cook we have encountered. I'm surprised there isn't anyone better here."

Julius lit up. "Oh, but there is! When the cook visited her family for a week, the daughter of *Herr* Weigand cooked such wonderful food! The bread was baked through and everything."

"So, why isn't she the cook?" Julius shrugged. He wondered the same thing.

Samuel spoke. "Cook hates cooking. She doesn't notice me. When no one else is there, she says it's a miserable job and she wants to garden." They both looked at him in surprise.

"Well, aren't you full of surprises, kiddo. You two boys may have just made life in this place a whole lot better for everyone." Raymond wanted to tousle the little lad's hair but was afraid of spooking him, so he settled for a giving him a friendly smile.

After an hour or two, Raymond fell asleep in the sunlit warmth of the garden and Bethel came out to join him. When he woke up, they discussed the situation.

"Judith became the cook when the old one simply left. The previous owner started investing in up-time things but the old cook believed the Ring of Fire was the work of the devil, so she left 'to save her soul'. Judith had been working in the kitchen some because she grew the herbs and vegetables, foraged for food, that sort of thing. They thought this made her the best person to the be the new cook without ever talking to her, and she hates the job. She knows she's bad at it. I think she's hoping if she's bad enough they'll send her back to the garden. But there isn't anyone else to take over."

"According to Julius and Samuel, the two little boys over there, there is someone! Werner's daughter is apparently an excellent cook. Perhaps we can request she cook for us?"

Bethel's stomach still wasn't settled from breakfast, so she wasted no time arranging this, leaving Judith with time to work in the garden she so loved.

After dinner, Werner approached them both. "Thank you. From the entire household, thank you, a thousand times over. Judith has asked to go back to being the gardener and my Hannah will be the cook. She mentioned liking to cook, but I did not realize she actually wished to *be* the cook. My personal thanks as well. Now Hannah will be able to earn money for her dowry and I can still keep an eye on her."

"Who are Samuel and Julius? My husband mentioned that they helped find the solution."

Werner's surprise showed through his professional poker face for a moment. "They are orphan children who help in exchange for a place to sleep and food. The one who is not right in the head has been working in the garden. I am not sure how much longer we can keep them here since Judith has returned to the garden. We do know how strongly up-timers feel about children being educated, but ones such as Samuel simply cannot be taught enough to be worth sending to school and Julius will not leave him, not even for school."

"Thank you, Werner. Please don't send them away. We would like to help make sure they can stay together and go somewhere safe."

Werner bowed. "Of course, *Frau* von Up-Time."

* * *

When they got to their room for the evening, Raymond regarded at his wife for a moment, then spoke before she had a chance. "Bethel, you don't have to say anything. At least, not to me. I know we're adopting the two boys and bringing them home with us." They had both wanted more children for so long, knowing they couldn't. Now that their two were grown and so many children were orphans, not adopting felt selfish. "I'll tell Brent and Bethel Ann, but you have to tell your family. I do *not* have that kind of spare time. We can talk to Julius and Samuel about it tomorrow, then find out their last names and how old they think they are."

"And if they're okay with us adopting them." Bethel prompted.

133

"Well, yes, if they are okay with leaving a life of drudgery to live in the magical town of Grantville."

"Not everyone sees it that way."

"Stop poking holes! You're getting what you want!"

Bethel grinned. "I get to have some fun at your expense." At that, Raymond grabbed her and spun her around until they both fell onto the bed laughing, too dizzy to stand.

CHAPTER 9

June 1633

"*Fraulein* Sagan, the librarians recommended you. They said you are part of the Cooking Club and an excellent researcher. I need help finding some recipes, so that makes you perfect. Specifically, I want to know how to make bagels and cream cheese as a surprise for my wife's birthday in October, so please keep this as secret as you can. If there are any ingredients or steps or tools that you don't recognize or that aren't available here, please ask me or do more research to find out what I can use. One thing I know we have is a liquid thermometer to check the temperature of milk, assuming it is heated to make cream cheese. We used it for hot chocolate when the kids were little. Do you think you can help me?" Raymond was having a hard time keeping the secret himself. He so wanted to tell Bethel about the project, but he wanted to save the surprise just a tiny bit more.

"*Ja*, I am the right researcher. My family owns a dairy farm, so I know a bit about making cheese and not only keeping it kosher." Seeing his expression, she burst out laughing. "My apologies, *Herr*

Little, but not all *Juden* are in money! Some of us must ensure we all have kosher food. However, I am sometimes tired of eating the same foods all the time. When my family agreed that I might come to Grantville to learn things, I took the chance to find new kosher foods. So, yes, I am skilled at finding ways to prepare food." *And being a good cook won't hurt my chances of finding a good husband, which is the real reason they sent me here. Not that I'm complaining. I did not want to marry anyone back home!*

When Raymond Little started belly-laughing, Rachel stood to leave, greatly offended. He managed to control himself enough to explain. "Please, wait! I think the ladies played a bit of a joke on both of us." He paused to wipe the tears from his eyes and control his breathing. "Up-time, the most famous and popular Jewish food was a bagel with cream cheese and lox, which is a kind of salmon, I think. By helping me, you may be bringing the most famous Jewish food of all time to your people a few centuries early."

Rachel's relief was apparent. She did not want to lose such a perfect research assignment. "I have heard of beygls. In Cracow, Poland, they give them to pregnant women. They are a round bread. Is this the same thing?"

"Could be. Bagels are a kind of round bread with a hole in the middle, small enough to hold in one hand. Almost positive they were boiled. I have no idea where they came from, but by 2000, Jewish people loved 'em. So did not-Jewish people. You can hear my stomach rumbling just thinking about eating bagels again. If you want to make cream cheese and bagels, you can learn along with us. Heck, maybe we'll open a bagel bakery together, *Fraulein*!" He wiggled his eyebrows and grinned, lest she take him seriously about opening a baker. He was a pharmacist, not a baker or entrepreneur.

July 1633

Jost Erhard gave a small prayer to steady his nerves. He didn't understand why the other smiths had turned down making the sock knitter. There were many parts, but the machine itself was simple enough. He had seen how much time his mother and sisters spent making and mending socks. Once women saw how it sped up the process, and how much longer it lasted than the cheaper wooden model, demand for the sock knitter would be as high as demand for the washing machine. Higher even, since individual households could afford a sock knitter but washing machines were often community purchases.

He felt blessed that Agatha had found him and now he had his masterwork. If they approved it, he would immediately start searching for a place to have his own smithy and for a way to mass-produce the sock knitters. As ready as he could be, Jost headed out to learn if he was approved as a master tinsmith.

* * *

"Congratulations, Master Erhard! This is a day to celebrate. *Frau Bauerin* and I have a present for you and Agatha. Used properly, this could ensure you have enough money to start your own smithy, and provide Agatha with an exceptionally healthy dowry." With that, a smiling Heinrich and Anna Maria handed them a letter in an up-time envelope, on up-time paper, written with an up-time pen.

Jost scanned the letter, then re-read the whole thing more closely before handing it to Agatha with a stunned expression. "Why? Why would *the* Doctor Nichols give us a letter saying he personally would like to see this business succeed? Why does a medical doctor care about *socks*? He even said that the military will probably buy them because Mike Stearns also cares about socks!" A common man, Jost was utterly unprepared for anything he did to ever receive notice from such lofty and important people, much less active help in the form of a letter of support. With this letter, he and Agatha could find people to help build a factory.

"When Agatha first found the sock knitter, she had a conversation with the good doctor about it. He said she needed to put something called an 'infomercial' on the television and he would make sure they aired it. She did one for the small sock knitter, but this is the machine Doctor Nichols had seen and liked. But even in Grantville, even with a successful business in the form of the small sock knitter, finding someone of means to take you seriously can be difficult for young people and Agatha had nothing in writing from Doctor Nichols. So, I talked to *Herr* Little, who works at Leahy, and he went to Doctor Nichols, and now you have a letter. I believe that if you look in the envelope again, Doctor Nichols had someone give you the names of a few towns that should welcome your little factory. You may need to be flexible, allow people to work half-days so they can tend to their fields or take pieces home to finish assembling them, that sort of thing. There are towns, such as these, that can use the work, provided you are willing to go a little farther from Grantville. If you get a good manager, you won't have to live there yourself, you can just visit."

Agatha wasn't shocked, but she was still very surprised. "Thank you, *Vatti*. Jost, when I talked to Doctor Nichols before, he told me that people with warm, dry feet stay healthier, and they need socks to do that. So, if we could find a way for people to make socks faster and cheaper, that would help them stay healthier. That is why the doctor wants the sock knitter to be 'mass produced' so much, and probably why Mike Stearns, the Prince of Germany, cares as well."

August 1633

Krystal gave a squeal of delight and hugged Sibylle Bauerin so tightly she dropped her bags onto the porch while her brother Johan laughed at them both. "Are you finally getting your eyes checked? How long will you be here? Where are you staying?"

"Yes, I have an appointment with Dr. Shipley next week. We don't know how long we will be here, but we're staying with Ursula for now. She invited us. Johan is here to keep me safe. Also, he will study up-time bread recipes," she glanced sideways at Krystal, "and possibly up-timers as well."

Krystal turned wave them both inside, which also hid the faint blush on her cheeks. "Johan, you should talk to Gisela. She is quite the baker and one of the founding members of the Grantville Cooking Club. She may be in the kitchen baking gingerbread houses right now. She does that a lot. My Aunt Anna was part of the club too. Last summer, she taught everyone in the club how to make mozzarella cheese! Her pie crusts were legendary. When she died, she left all her kitchen gadgets to the Club. She left her cookbooks to Gisella, but I think that was mostly to tick off Grannie B and Aunt Bethel. Laugh's on her: neither one cared. Gisela is oddly passionate about gingerbread. Personally, I'm getting a bit sick of the stuff, but that's what happens when you live with a baker focused on 'perfecting' a recipe. Am I right Sibylle?" Seeing that Sibylle and Johan practically had their heads on a swivel looking around the up-time living room, she stopped trying to chat and gave them The Grand Tour. Johan's Grand Tour of an Up-Time House went through the dining room and stopped dead in the kitchen. Unlike her brother, Sibylle's Grand Tour of an Up-Time House included the whole house, except the attic. With her poor eyesight, she couldn't see anything up there.

* * *

"*Vatti*, can you carve some wooden gingerbread molds for my houses?" Gisela was tired of Margaretha's bugging her to ask. Worse yet, she had realized by two months ago that Margaretha was right, she just couldn't quite bring herself to admit it and ask him. Now Johan was visiting and one of his first questions was where she planned to get gingerbread molds for the houses. She was too embarrassed to admit her pride had kept her from asking her own family, so here she was. Asking.

"*Meine geliebte Tochter,* why would you need such a thing from me? Since you haven't asked in all these many months, I thought you must have found a better craftsman than your old *Vatti* to help your new business." Heinrich's hangdog expression made Gisela realize she should have asked him months ago. Margaretha was right. Again. It was a nasty habit of hers.

Her shoulders slumped. "I'm sorry, *Vatti*. I haven't asked anyone else. I just…. I guess I just didn't think we needed them yet. I didn't want to pester you the way Margaretha has been pestering me."

He gave her a hug and a smile. "My not-so-little girl, give me a minute." True to his word, a minute later, he returned and, with a bow and a flourish of his hand, presented her with the same up-time grocery bag Mrs. Flannery had given her *Mutti*.

Gisela peeked in, then gasped and started pulling things out. "How did you know? They are perfect!" The bag was filled with carved molds for walls, roofs, chimneys, and all manner of house parts.

"You aren't the only one Margaretha can pester." Seeing Gisela's shock that Margaretha would pester a master craftsman about something so unimportant, he winked. "No, not me. Tyrone is sweet on Margaretha. When I found out what my journeyman was doing in his spare time, of course I started as well. In fact, this convinces us that we should start selling small gingerbread molds in our own store alongside the angels and other small items. It is good to be practicing my true craft again. So few people here purchase gingerbread molds. As you like to say, there are no guilds here to stop us from doing what is most profitable for us!"

As she pulled the final mold from the bag and hugged her father, Gisela turned the mold upside down. Pieces from it slipped out onto the floor, leaving her with nothing in her hand but a nearly empty frame with one stuck piece, her mouth a perfect O of surprise.

"And now you see the real surprise for you! Tyrone pointed out that you will want the ability to make each building look different from the others. These molds are like puzzles, and worthy of being a masterwork. You swap out the tiles to have different windows, brick or wood and plaster, fancy or plain doors, however you want to imagine it. Once it's set, you tighten the sides on the frame, then roll your dough out. We can stick to the regular style, if you prefer, or make more of these. But we don't plan on selling these, or even letting other people know they exist. These are a special gift for my not-so-little girl, who should keep them as a trade secret. Let the other bakers wonder how you do it!"

Gisela looked intently at the new gingerbread forms, then startled her father by suddenly yelling. "Margaretha! Come in here quick! Bring Johan if he's here." They spent the next two hours talking to Heinrich and Tyrone, playing with the new forms, and coming up with ideas for more.

September 1633

This year, Bethel was humming with a spring in her step as she stopped by the now-annual Gardens event known as *The Most Wonderful Day Breakfast*. Her up-time kids had both graduated, but their newly adopted sons were both duly enrolled in elementary school. She wanted to meet some of the other parents with young children. Julius (eight) and Samuel (five) needed more friends to play with.

Liesl found her first. "It's been months! Everyone at the Cooking Club misses you. Your new business must be keeping you busy."

"Well, there's that, and my day job, but I guess you didn't hear. We adopted two boys a few months ago! Julius is eight and Samuel is five. We always wanted more kids, so Raymond and I are ecstatic about it."

Liesl looked torn. She wanted to be happy for her friend, but she was worried. "That's great, but how do you have two jobs plus two small children? Did you hire help? Please tell me you hired help."

"Oh, right. We found them living in a hunting lodge Thomas Nehring owns. A widow named Hette Treutmann lived there and had become fond of the boys. Since the feeling was mutual, we brought her with them. You've seen our house. We did not have space for three more people, even with two of them being little people. So, we built a little house in the backyard for Bethel Ann and Brent to live in. Of course, they still use the shower and kitchen in the main house on a regular basis, but at least they have more privacy. Samuel loves those little closets under the eaves. He has his own personal space there where he can go when he needs to, which is really important."

"Why so much more important for Samuel, Bethel?"

"Samuel has Down's Syndrome. It does a lot of different things to a person, but the ones you would recognize are that they look different and they aren't good at book-learning and school. They are, however, almost always incredibly kind and caring. Sweet. My Mom used to say they were angels come down to help us. That's how Samuel is."

"That is a *lot* for one person to take on. You need to have a beer, and not a small beer either, and go talk to all your friends. Right now! If I don't see you at a Cooking Club meeting soon, I'll go find this Hette Treutmann of yours and get her to make you go."

Bethel threw her hands up in mock surrender. "I'll do it! I promise!"

"You better! We bought the land for the cooking school, now we need to decide the rest of the details. I need another voice of sanity in the room. Some of those proposals are downright crazy."

✳ ✳ ✳

Raymond was apprehensive. He loved his wife, but baking was not his forte and his new job at Leahy left him with almost no free time. "Ladies I will follow your lead. I want to help make these bagels for Bethel, but reading this recipe, I'm glad we have plenty of time to work out any problems before her birthday in October." As a pharmacist, compounding ingredients was part of Raymond's job. As sixteenth century pharmacist, he was an herbalist too, so he had to do exacting measuring and mixing of ingredients all day long. Now, as the Chief Pharmacist at Leahy Medical Center, he had to find the ingredients for other people to make medicines all day. Baking had to be easier than that. Didn't it? He was nervous.

"Rachel, Uncle Raymond isn't much of a cook. Neither am I, for that matter, but Gisela here, and her mother, are both regular gourmets, so we're hoping they'll help us through the rough bits." Gisela and Anna Maria soon shooed Krystal away from the actual cooking and focused her on finding things they needed, like a giant pot to boil the bagels and cheesecloth for draining whey from the cream cheese when they got there. Despite Raymond's lack of baking experience, his pharmacy experience made him a natural, at least for measuring and mixing.

Gisela loved baking, but she wasn't experimental like Effi Schuetzin. She liked variations on things she already understood. Something as radically different as bread that was boiled made her nervous. *I do not understand why anyone would boil bread. This does not make sense. We must bake a few without boiling them first to see how they are.* Gisela did not even discuss the matter with anyone, she simply put several bagels in the oven before they could be boiled.

Hungry from the baking and the anticipation, Gisela, Raymond, and Rachel dug into the first, ugly, unboiled bagels with butter while they waited for the boiled ones to bake. Every single one fell apart where the ends overlapped, and even the down-timers who had never eaten a bagel before could tell something was off. The up-timers didn't even finish theirs. They just weren't bagels. They weren't even very good bread. The boiled batch was clearly better, although they also fell apart and lacked the special something that makes a bagel a bagel. Lesson learned: never skip boiling the bagels.

Everyone went back to the recipes in search of the missing ingredient or step. "The boiling!" Everyone looked up at Krystal's exclamation. "This note says it's more than putting them in boiling water. Did you add baking soda when you boiled the bagels? I don't remember anyone asking me to find baking soda while you were baking, and I didn't see any on the counter earlier."

Gisela acted slightly guilty. "I did not. I thought the writer made a mistake. Who puts baking soda in water? No one, that's who. Why does the water need baking soda? It doesn't need to rise!" She looked exceedingly put out by this, especially since no one had an answer for her. Knowing that she had caused them to waste half a batch of bagels by her refusal to boil them didn't help her attitude.

Krystal shrugged. "I'm not a baker, obviously, but it's the only thing any of us found so we need to try another batch with baking soda in the water, and we boil *all* the bagels this time." Raymond had to leave for work, but with that discovery, everyone else was back on the case, making a second batch of bagels. They were still ugly, and the ends still came apart, but they tasted better. This time, they realized they hadn't finished the bagels with an egg wash for a lovely golden glow. The up-timers pronounced the third batch "almost as good as Lender's" and the down-timers fell in love.

From what little Krystal and Raymond could remember, they weren't in the same league as fresh-baked bagels from a bagel bakery and Gisela wasn't entirely satisfied either, despite never having had one before, so she kept tinkering, trying to perfect the bagels. She tried so hard that she almost spoiled the secret when her family started carrying bagels for lunch and people got curious. After that, she cut down on how many she was making, but she had the recipe almost nailed by then.

✻ ✻ ✻

Rachel was nervous as she walked into Krystal's kitchen. Today, they were making cream cheese for the first time as well as another batch of bagels. "*Herr* Little, I found a cheesemaker to help. The Cow Barnes wants to make cream cheese to add to their cheese selection once we have the recipe. If this works, I will teach them and they will make larger batches for us."

Raymond nodded. "Anissa runs a solid operation out there. I got fresh cream and milk from them this morning. With the vinegar and salt on hand, we have everything we need for at least one batch of cream cheese, probably two. We're getting low on vinegar, though." Three hours later, the whey was draining off the first batch of cream cheese and the bagels were going into the oven.

"*Frau* Treutmann can make vinegar for you. Ask her. Will this cream cheese truly be ready tomorrow? Most cheese takes months or even years to be ready to eat." Gisela was clearly a Doubting Thomas about cream cheese. "You are sure the cheese is just supposed to be on the counter overnight for one night? That seems too simple." Her list of concerns felt never-ending.

Rachel reassured her. "It makes me nervous too, but the recipe was quite clear. We will know tomorrow, after the cream cheese is finished and the up-timers tell us if it tastes right. I hope it does! I want to try making another 'fast cheese' I found called 'paneer' from India." Since they weren't professional bakers, their arms were too tired from kneading to make another batch of bagels that day. They agreed to meet at Raymond's office the next day at lunch to try the bagels with cream cheese. Very nearly a professional baker, Gisela

147

volunteered to make a batch of bagels in the morning and bring everything to his office.

Krystal spoke. "What do you all think about bringing everything in a cooler? Then no one should be able to smell the fresh bread smell as you are walking."

Raymond shook his head. "I think more people would be curious about what's so special it needs an up-time cooler. Lots of people eat fresh bread now, so the smell doesn't attract much attention. Using a regular basket or bag or whatever you ladies carry now should be fine. Just keep it well covered! We're so close, I don't want to ruin the surprise, and I don't want to share the bagels *or* the cream cheese."

The next day at lunch, Krystal and Raymond pronounced the cream cheese "excellent but tarter than Philly." The bagels themselves were noticeably prettier than the first batches. They didn't fall apart at the ends anymore and they were uniform all the way around, thanks to Gisela. They probably wouldn't have won accolades in New York City, but they were darn tasty bagels and, after the year he and Bethel had just gone through, Raymond felt it was the best money he had ever spent. He hadn't simply put money into her present, he had put time and thought into her gift. (No need to mention how much he had enjoyed sampling the test batches.)

October 1633

On Bethel's birthday, the last batch of cream cheese was safely (and carefully) hidden in Krystal's fridge, previous batches having disappeared quickly. Raymond fervently hoped the current batch—

the one with dehydrated berries mixed in—had turned out well. When he left home that morning to make a final batch of bagels and get the cream cheeses, Raymond left a note for Bethel.

Honey, I'll be back in a few hours with your birthday gift, so don't go far. I'm going to be bringing breakfast, maybe lunch, so don't eat too much. Just call it a birthday brunch! I hope you enjoy your gift! — R

Raymond removed his jacket as he walked into Krystal's kitchen and saw everything neatly laid out to start baking, including aprons. "Gisela, you didn't need to wake up so early to help me with this! Well, I guess not so early for you, but still, thank you."

She smiled. "If I help, then I can eat bagels, too, and I want bagels. I make extra for my family."

Rachel clearly heard the comment as she walked in, grinning. "Yes, wanting to eat bagels every day is easy! I can understand why *Frau* Little missed them."

Three hours after he left, Raymond walked back into his house to find his dangerously hangry wife glaring at him and *Frau* Treutmann shooing Julius and Samuel outside to play. "I just need one minute in the kitchen, honey. I promise I wasn't at work. Today is all about you. Just one minute. It's worth the wait." He wasn't a newlywed. He kept moving while he talked, pulling out a plate and utensils, checking to make sure she had coffee. "Another thirty seconds. That's all I need." Plucking a bagel from his bag of fresh bagels, slicing it, then putting the open bagel on a plate. "Fifteen seconds." Putting a small knife in each cream cheese, all while she glared a hole in him from her seat at the table, still not having seen what he thought was so special that it was worth going hungry all morning.

Quickly arranging everything on a decorative tray. "Almost ready." He covered the plate and cream cheese with a tea towel. "Okay. It's done." He placed the tray in front of her. "Happy birthday, my love!" With a flourish, he uncovered the bagel and cream cheese.

Her squeal of glee was all he had hoped for. Bethel jumped up and hugged him. "You found bagels! And cream cheese! How did you manage it? Where did you find them? I was sure we didn't even have recipes for either one down-time!" She sat down again, coated the bagel with cream cheese, plain on one half and berry on the other, and started chowing down, oblivious to everything but her breakfast.

"I hired a researcher to find the recipes, and then worked with Krystal," seeing her disbelieving expression, he smiled and continued, "and Gisela to make them for you. Krystal found things we needed to bake in the house. Happy birthday, honey." Her expression, and the mmm'ing sounds she made as she ate first one, then a second, and considered a third before deciding to at least pause, made the answer clear. His present was a success!

November 1633

A few weeks after Bethel's birthday, Rachel called on the family. "I wish to discuss something with you. Being in Grantville, it is hard to not want to start a business. This is a business I would like to start. A café selling bagels, cream cheese, and coffee will do very well. People who want their food quickly on their way to work will love it. My family can help with the cost to start, and with getting coffee beans, but starting this without asking you to be partners would not be right. Such a café will make much money. When the time comes, my family and their friends will help us start branches in many cities, and they will all send us some of the profit after we send them the recipes and business plan. We would not know of these bagels and cream cheese without you. Of course, up-timers usually bring more ideas, and more profit, to their business partners, even when they are 'silent partners'. My family agrees and likes this plan for business." When she finished, Rachel sat looking nervously at them, silently waiting for their judgment.

Raymond acted uncomfortable. "Rachel, making bagels for my family was great and all, but I'm too busy at Leahy to help start a business. I can barely carve out time to spend with Bethel and the kids. I'm really sorry, but I will definitely be a customer!"

Rachel looked disappointed until Bethel started speaking. "My job keeps me busy, but it's not interesting. Someone else could easily do the work now. I'm basically a tax collector and I...do not love being a tax collector. No sane person loves being a tax collector. Perhaps we can build a business together, Rachel. A bagel café might be fun. A lot of work, and painfully early mornings, but fun. Especially compared to being a tax collector. I have never once seen a person happy about paying taxes."

"Why 'painfully early'?" Rachel was curious.

"Up-time, bagels were a breakfast food, sometimes lunch. But not dinner. So, bagel bakeries opened early, and closed early. Not just sunrise-early, bakery early, early enough that the first bagels are coming out of the oven ready to eat at sunrise. Because they opened so early, they usually closed shortly after lunch.

Raymond had never seen Bethel this genuinely interested in anything related to a job for herself. "Bethel isn't a morning person, so she must like the idea a lot. So, how do you know so much about bagel bakeries, oh love of my life?"

"Morgantown. Whenever I went shopping in Morgantown, I went to this little bagel bakery there, but the first two times I tried, they were already closed for the day. The third time, they were almost out of bagels. When I finally got there early enough, I asked why they opened and closed so early, and the answer stuck with me. Rachel, what do you think?"

"Yes! But there is one more thing to address. *Herr* Little talked about 'bagels with cream cheese' being a Jewish food up-time, but here-and-now, 'Jewish' food will not sell well. You must be mindful of this and not say it is Jewish food."

"You're right and we won't market this as a Jewish food, but kosher kitchens are generally cleaner, which makes them healthier. They are slowly becoming known for that, so I'm happy to use that as a reason to have Jews cooking. Up-timers have become well known for our odd attachment to cleanliness, so people will accept a kosher kitchen, and *Juden* cooking for them, more easily from an up-time café. Hmmm. I see what you mean about having an up-timer involved helping." Bethel liked the idea more and more. "We haven't sold many of our things or spent much money since we came here. The house and pharmacy mortgages were both left behind, along with Raymond's partner in the business and his entire family, so our expenses are low. Yes, Raymond and I will talk about it a bit more first, but I think we might be able to invest and start a bagel café with you. Once we have one up and going, if all goes well, we can talk about how and if we should expand beyond Grantville."

December 1633

To her surprise, Sarah Jane had found she enjoyed being on the TV show. Most of the time, people never saw the hard work she put into her cooking or how beautiful food could be. "It's hard to believe it's that time of year again, but we have another potato treat in store for you. Potato pancakes! They're also called latkes, and yes, for those of you who are already asking, that is a Jewish word. We've said it before, we'll say it again: eating Jewish food doesn't make you Jewish any more than eating Catholic food makes you Catholic or Lutheran food makes you Lutheran. If that's the way the world worked, princes wouldn't need invading armies to change people's religion. They'd just send out the cooks! Plus, most people just called 'em potato pancakes."

Effi took her turn. "Before we start cooking, there is a question we have gotten a lot the last two weeks. What, exactly, is the small building in the background on our set? It's an up-time tradition called a 'gingerbread house' and, like the name says, it's a house made of baked gingerbread, like the cookies. Our own Gisela Schulte made that model of a new cooking school we hope to open in the next few years. The city of Grantville also commissioned her to make a gingerbread house replica of Calvert High School for the royal family, in the person of Princess Kristina, as a Christmas gift from the State of Thuringia.

"Now, back to the latkes! They are simple. Shredded potatoes, onions, and egg, Add a touch of flour and salt. Fry them. Easy as pie! Or perhaps we should start saying, easy as latkes!

"Now, let's get cooking!"

PART 4: 1634

Bethanne Kim

CHAPTER 10

January 1634

Rachel was nervous. Bethel was nervous. Gisela was nervous. Even Raymond was nervous, and he wasn't technically an owner or an employee. Basically, everyone involved was nervous. The next morning was the grand opening of "Up-Time Bagels & Cream Cheese", the newest Grantville eatery. Technically, they were still a catering company delivering to the Gardens, grocery stores, and other places to get people excited about bagels. Rachel and Bethel owned the company and Gisela was their head bagel baker.

It didn't take long. Everyone sold out by noon and asked for more bagels and cream cheese, but especially bagels. Over three centuries early, a bagel was the latest breakfast craze. Two days later, they hired an apprentice bagel baker. The day after that, they signed a contract with Anissa at the Cow Barnes for cream cheese and started searching for a journeyman to add to the staff. By the end of the month, they were searching for a storefront. And searching, and searching. Three times, they thought they finally had a storefront to use. Once, they were outbid. Once, the tenant decided to stay. Once, the tenant kept the lease and sublet the place to a relative. Frustrating didn't begin to describe the situation.

"Honey, I don't know what to do. I still think of Grantville as a backwater hick town with half of the storefronts vacant, but as soon as something comes up, it's rented like that." Bethel snapped her fingers. "Rachel and I really want to open a storefront. I can't speak for her, but I'm about ready to give up. We have two little boys now and the catering business, plus my job. I don't have time for this on top of everything else!"

"How about good ol' Dick Head? He owns a lot of properties. Did you ask him if you could rent any?"

Bethel swatted him. "*Jimmy Dick* doesn't manage his own properties and yes, I talked to his property manager, but they are all occupied right now. Bunny promised to give us a heads up if anything comes available, but I didn't get a good feeling from her. Demand is too high." Bunny Lamb was one of the best-connected realtors and property managers in Grantville. She seemed to know the moment a person started thinking about selling or renting a property.

"I wish we could help you out with space in the pharmacy, but the best we could do is sell some of your bagels and cream cheese like other places do. We don't have any unused space, either. We might be able to remodel that shed out back and make a little shop for you there, but I can't make that call without talking to John first. He's the one who still works there every day, and I won't go waltzing in and making changes on him. With all the stuff behind the shop, we couldn't make anything very big for you. Even the old lunch counter is crammed since Ursula turned it into our herbal dispensary."

Bethel lit up. "The old lunch counter! That's perfect! It's beyond perfect." She grabbed his face in both hands and gave him a long kiss that temporarily distracted him and made him forget his main objection. "I forgot that was there!"

His eyes unfocused for a minute as he gathered the threads of his lost train of thought. "But we're already using that space, so you can't use it. How is an unavailable space better than a newly remodeled space behind the store?"

"Silly man. You tear down the shed, build a new space, and move the herbal remedies there. I see how hard working in there is for all of you. The layout is all wrong, you need more drawers, the counter seats are in the way, and there isn't enough light, for starters. Not to mention how inconvenient having the grill and other restaurant equipment there is. The new space can be purpose-built and absolutely perfect for herbalists, just like the old lunch counter will be perfect for us. If you make sure there are enough windows to fill the space in natural light and drawers of all sizes all over the place, the herbalists will be happy as pigs in clover. Then we can use the lunch counter for food service! I'm going to go tell Corinne right now. She's the one who got me to try that bagel shop in Morgantown, so she'll be on board, and I know she'll get John to agree. No sensible man will block his wife on something like this!"

Being a sensible man himself, Raymond waved goodbye as Bethel bundled up and headed over to see Corinne, and no doubt Rachel and Gisella after that. Recognizing Moss and Little's Cut Rate

Pharmacy was about to start a construction project, he heaved a mental sigh that would've blown the front door off its hinges if it had been a real sigh. He could fight it, John could fight it, but he knew that in the end, they were building something out back so his wife could sell bagels and cream cheese at the lunch counter, and John's wife could eat them there. It was just a matter of how long the build-out took, and how expensive the whole project ended up becoming. He had a sneaking suspicion that somehow, some way, they were going to end up with a full bakery out back, too, but he tried to put that down to paranoia.

February 1634

Anna Maria patted the sofa beside her and motioned for Krystal to sit and talk, or, more accurately, listen. "Krystal, our family has decided to leave Grantville after Agatha graduates. You and Sam are both moving on with your lives in other places. We know how expensive rent is here, and that our rent is unchanged since we moved in that first summer. You and Grandpa Eli should receive the full market rate, but we cannot pay more and still expand Heinrich's business, or mine. Plus, we cannot pay for the additional business space we need in Grantville. We will leave shortly before you move to Jena.

"We know how much you worry, but we have a plan. Gisela has spent much of her free time in the library researching places our relatives live, looking for opportunities. She discovered that Lauscha, where Heinrich's cousins live, will become famous in two hundred years for making glass Christmas tree ornaments. The Duke of

THE GOURMETS OF GRANTVILLE

Saxony-Coburg gave two glassblowers permission to start the village of Lauscha about forty years ago. The area includes everything needed to make glass and the Duke wanted his own glassmaker nearby. Gisela found information on how glassblowers of the future made these ornaments, and we are taking it to them. She even picked up a few pieces of broken ornaments as examples. They could become quite a fad with the nobility.

"When Heinrich wrote them of the glass Christmas ornaments in Grantville, the town was so excited they voted to change their name. Unfortunately, they chose three different names and are still wrangling to decide the final one, but every name includes 'Christmas' somehow. They hope for this to make them a much bigger, more prosperous town, but it is still a town in the 'hills and hollers' of the Thuringerwald, and they don't actually want a ton of tourists. Just their money. Plus, people are still afraid to go into the Thuringerwald since it isn't exactly the safest place around. So, we are going to help them find a solution."

Krystal swallowed her sadness. "I understand. You must do what's best for your family. I will miss you all, but I get it, I am leaving this summer. Probably by early July. You're right, it's good timing. I definitely want to visit this glassblowing town, though. I always liked seeing glassblowing when I got to go to an up-time Ren Faire. Perhaps I can convince the Red Cross to visit with the traveling clinic." They both were quiet for a minute before Krystal spoke again. "You've been saying it for ages, and you're right. I need to stop thinking of this as Grannie B and Grandpa Eli's home and start thinking of it as a way to earn money. Bunny Lamb takes care of

Sam's properties. She can take care of this one too. I'll empty out my room, too, so she can rent out the whole house."

"Will you stay at the Higgins or the Inn of the Maddened Queen when you visit?"

"Neither one, Anna Maria. Tyrone will be going with you, I assume, unless Margaretha stays here. I'll use that little room we made for him. I can lock it up tight while I'm gone so I don't have to worry about my stuff. Plus, I don't want to be stressed about finding a room when I visit. I guess that's it, then. We have a plan, and we'll all be out by mid-summer."

"We'll all miss you. Please do visit us. I expect Lauscha to be about as exciting as you say Grantville was before the Ring of Fire, but you're still welcome. Now, you need to get going to classes before you are late. Shoo!"

March 1634

The choir room on the first floor of the church was always a bit cool, with the bulk of the sanctuary overhead and thick stone walls insulating it. Linda dropped her purse on a chair along with her coat and put on a thinner, boiled wool jacket she wore for practicing and the start of choir rehearsals. By the end of rehearsal, the choir room was usually toasty. Even up-time, no parish fully heated their sanctuary, and the downstairs rooms could be a bit nippy, and that was before they were in The Little Ice Age. Funds only stretched so far. So, Linda kept her boiled wool jacket in the choir room for practicing and wore it under her robe during particularly cold services.

Allowing her mind to wander while her hands warmed up playing tunes she had known since high school, she realized that St. Mary's had file cabinets full of music. She'd always known that, of course, but it hit her in a way it somehow hadn't before. A few down-timers had poked around in the cabinets, but she hadn't, not really, not in years and years, and she had never looked closely at the oldest music. Church Music Directors rarely got rid of old music because you never knew when the budget would get cut and you couldn't buy more, so there was bound to be some truly old stuff, possibly from before the mines started dying and people started leaving Grantville after WWII. Resolved to find some good new-old music for the choir to try, Linda stopped playing and walked to the back of the room to the start looking.

Startled to see a person crumpled on the floor next to the cabinets, Linda let out a yell and jumped back, knocking over chairs and falling into the resulting mess in the process. Hearing the ruckus, Father Gus' wife Hannelore rushed in. "*Frau* Bartolli! Are you hurt? What is happened?"

Linda stood, wincing and brushing herself off. "No lasting damage to me, but I think I may have a few bruises to explain for the next week or so. Worse, though, I may have broken the spine and damaged some of the pages on that hymnal," gesturing at one particularly rumpled looking hymnal lying right where she had land.

"What happened?"

"My darling daughter happened. She was next to the cabinets, curled up on the floor looking half-dead, which she apparently isn't.

Since the door was locked when I came in, I didn't expect anyone to be in here and she scared the bejeebers out of me."

Hannelore looked sheepish. "That is my fault. When I saw her at the door, I unlocked it and left her in. Since she is your daughter, I thought you expected her."

After all the commotion, Tina was sitting on the floor with her back against the filing cabinets, carefully situated between two rows so the drawer pulls didn't cut into her back. "It's my fault. I locked the door to be left alone. I didn't even register that today is choir practice. I needed to be somewhere that felt safe, and somewhere I wouldn't have to talk to Greg or the kids for a bit." Hearing Tina's tiny voice and words, Hannelore slipped out and locked the door to give the mother and daughter privacy. Everyone knew Tina was deathly ill. Even if they didn't, looking at her gave it away. Down-timers were no strangers to the need for people to grieve their own impending passage as their time drew near.

"Mom, I saw the doctor this morning. He said I have less than a year, more likely six months. Six months! Christina is barely six. Little Jimmy is only three. They'll never remember me. They won't even have a decent picture of me. I'm not sure I want them to remember me like this, but I don't know what they'll think if all they have are pictures of me from before the Ring of Fire. I'll say it. I was fat. Obese. The picture of a diabetic well on her way to a heart attack. A disgusting pig who ate so much crap, and drank so much soda, I destroyed my own body. It was so easy, Mom! One cheese doodle turning into a whole bag. A small glass of soda one day. Another day I needed a bigger caffeine boost and a small turned into a medium, then a large. On bad days, I drank straight from the two-liter bottle. Finished the whole thing myself, a few times." Tears leaked down her cheeks. "Greg hated it when I did that, but staying awake with a little kid and a job was so hard some days. It never felt like a big deal."

Linda and Tina sat in silence for a minute until Tina continued. "I remember the first time I had a cigarette. A classmate dared me when I was twelve. Did you know that? Twelve. I hated the taste and how it made me feel, but I didn't want to look like a little kid. By the time I didn't care, I was hooked."

The bitterness in her voice shocked Linda. She knew her daughter had started smoking, or at least hanging out with smokers, in middle school. The smell was unmistakable, but she and Greg had never figured out how to broach the subject, and they were never absolutely sure she was the one smoking. Uncertain what to say, Linda did what moms have always done when their children hurt. She sat down next to her and hugged her baby, listening while she poured out her woes.

"I've never understood it, Mom. Why me? And why couldn't the Ring of Fire have happened after my surgery? It was only a few weeks. After we came back here, we all lost weight and changed our diets since we didn't have a choice. If they had fixed my heart before we came here, I would have more time with Greg and the kids. More time to help people down here. It's horrible. Being a nurse, knowing how much I could help people here-and-now, if I wasn't so sick that I can't even help myself. I can't blame anyone but myself. It's awful." Neither one ever knew how long they sat there, Tina's head on

Linda's shoulder while Linda stroked her hair and Tina slowly calmed down.

"Thank you, Mom. I feel better now. Greg and I can talk. The kids are too young to understand much, but we'll figure something out. Do you know why I came here?" Linda shook her head no. "When we were kids, you would bring us here while you practiced and if no one else could watch us during choir practice. I was out of the way back here, and the cabinets were so smooth and cool to lean against in the summer. Sometimes, I opened the drawers and looked through them, but I never found anything interesting. Just lots of music. So many copies of the same music, and most of it printed before you and Dad were born. I could sit back here and read, or color, or whatever. If I was quiet and didn't leave a mess, no one bothered me. No one noticed me. No one asked a thing of me. I sat here and daydreamed.

"This is also where I learned to open candy bars and candy bags silently, which is almost impossible to do. When I had to write my college admissions essays about why I wanted to be a nurse, I came here. The church secretary let me in since I'm your daughter. I sat here, leaning against these filing cabinets, and wrote out my dreams for being a nurse and helping the world." Tina moved away and sat leaning against the cabinets again. She gave a bitter laugh. "Look at me now. 'Helping the world!' I can't even help my own family.

"Sometime during college, I stopped coming in this room much. I couldn't fit in between the cabinets handles anymore and that just emphasized how fat I had gotten. It hurt. It hurt my body, and it hurt my heart. Do you remember when I pulled out all those old dresses from the attic in '32? The ones from high school, before I got so damn fat? And don't tell me I wasn't, or that I 'was beautiful'. I know you, Dad, Greg, the kids, the family, love me no matter how I look. That doesn't change that I weighed too damn much. One Sunday in '32, I realized I could fit between the cabinet handles again and that afternoon, I went home and pulled out all that old clothing. Wearing those old jeans again felt so *good!* But the damage was done, and now I have less than a year to live. So, what should I do, Mom?"

Sometimes Linda missed the days when a hug and kiss would heal her children's owies. "You keep planning for them, honey. You already have someone helping with the kids and a housekeeper and her husband to help with the house and yard. The kids will have someone they already know to take care of them when the time comes, so make sure you keep them all. I know you worry about the cost, but Greg will need them all and you can afford it. This is 1634. Having staff is *normal,* even for completely healthy people. Remember what Beulah and Garnet talked to you about: teaching others, creating syllabi, and writing teaching aids for nursing students is a way for you to 'help the world' and you know it's true.

"If you want to help even more, find someone strong to help you, *just* you. Train whoever you find as a home care assistant who can go train others when you are gone. Preferably a woman so there isn't any embarrassment if you need help getting dressed or that sort of thing. You will still be helping with your nursing knowledge in a different way. You know it's something no one else has had time to do, if they even think about it, and it's something that's needed."

"Thanks, Mom. That does help."

Linda leaned forward and brushed her daughter's hair back. "Now, I think it's time for you to go home. The parish bought a small rickshaw to help parishioners who aren't feeling well get home. I am declaring that you qualify! You might want to buy one for your own use, if you can find one. Demand is surprisingly high. Greg can use it with the kids for at least the next decade. Let's find Hannelore and she'll rustle up someone to take you home while I finish getting ready for choir practice tonight."

As she watched the rickshaw pull away from St. Mary's with her daughter, Linda whispered to herself as she leaned against the door jam, sweater wrapped tightly around herself, "You have always been beautiful to me, my little girl."

April 1634

"Phil, what can we do? Married woman and mother or not, Tina is still our little girl, and we won't have her much longer. I want to do something special, but flying to Italy, or anywhere else, is out with her health being so bad." Linda and Phil had had years to accept that they would outlive their daughter, but that didn't make watching her fade away any easier.

"Since you told me about her most recent prognosis last month, I've been thinking on exactly that. There is only one thing for you to do, and only you can do this. You need to put together a program of her favorite organ music and perform those pieces for her. All of them, including *Sunrise, Sunset.* Don't think I missed you playing that for her on the piano at home for all those years! The other two kids have their own songs, but that one is hers. As a matter of fact, play it first."

"Really? That would be a lot of work and I'm sure there is something she would like more than just to hear me play. Plus, *Sunrise, Sunset* is about an arranged Jewish marriage, which would be kind of weird."

"No. That's it. Greg told me she found an old cassette of you practicing when she was in high school. She listens to you playing on her worst days. Pay someone to rewrite part of the lyrics for *Sunrise, Sunset.* I bet Trommler will record the whole performance and sell copies. We don't need the money and Greg and the kids are good, so the profits could go to something for medical care. Maybe a nursing scholarship or something like that? We'll need to talk to her about what she wants, unless you want to try to keep it a secret?"

"No, not a secret. You convinced me, plus that would be a hard secret to keep. For someone that sick, having something to look forward to is good for their health, and she can help me choose the music. But let's keep the *Sunrise, Sunset* rewrite a secret."

＊ ＊ ＊

"Finding a construction company in a boom town like Grantville is easy. Finding a good one? Not so easy. Finding a good one available to work soon? Almost impossible. *Almost.*" Raymond started sipping his coffee, waiting for Bethel to prod him for the information.

"Well? How did you manage this miracle? Spill."

"Construction workers start work early. They like cheap, hearty, easy-to-carry breakfasts, preferably warm and accompanied by coffee. They will get breakfast daily while working on site for up to two weeks, a twenty percent discount for the first month it's open, ten percent for the rest of the first year, and the foreman gets a pound of cream cheese. And you, my lovely wife, get a bakery and storefront. Now what do I get?" He grinned lazily at her.

"Bagels, cream cheese, and coffee on demand. And cheesecake on your birthday."

"Hey! That's not fair. Why not cheesecake every day?"

"What do you think we're made of, money? Cheesecake was expensive even up-time! Besides, I'll have every doctor in town after me if I start giving you cheesecake daily. There is also the tiny detail that we don't quite *have* cheesecake yet." She hugged him and stared deep into his eyes. "But truly, thank you. We didn't expect to get the bakery until, well, we had no idea when, but not this year. You came through for us in a big way."

Still holding onto his wife, Raymond sat and settled her onto his leg so they could continue talking and snuggling. "Something came up while I was talking to the builders. Someone is selling quesadillas and burritos from a lunch cart, and his guys love them. Do you think Gisela or one of the other bakers could make tortillas?"

"Hmm. I want to say yes, I mean really, little old abuelas made them, so how hard can they be? And you're telling me someone else is already making them. But I had a Spanish class about five hundred years ago and I seem to remember that Mexicans used a special kind of flour we don't have. Something about the corn perhaps? I don't know. I can talk to Anita and see if she knows anything. As focused as Gisela is on perfecting bagel baking, don't expect much soon. Looking at the time, perhaps we should go check out the not-quite competition for lunch?"

Raymond's stomach let out a giant gurgle right then. "That would be a yes, ma'am! I don't know about you, but I did not know I missed burritos and quesadillas until I heard about the lunch cart. Now, if they are any good, I'll have one every day this week!"

May 1634

The mechanics of getting their first cafe up and running preoccupied Bethel and Gisela for months, especially finding a location. Every week, Rachel pulled them out of their current preoccupation for a business meeting. When Rachel arrived at the bakery for a weekly meeting in May and found Gisela waiting for it to start, she wasn't sure how to act, so she brought Bethel in and poured them each a coffee before sitting.

Gisela was determined to share her idea with both founders of *The Up-Time Bagel & Cream Cheese Company* before her nerves failed her. "You know my family is leaving for Lauscha next month. I do not know how long they will stay there, but I already worried that I would not find a husband in such a small, remote village and now I have learned that most of the young men are marrying the daughters of local woodsmen. I truly do not wish to live in Lauscha, but my family is moving there. My parents agree that finding a suitable suitor for me in Lauscha may be challenging." Making the ask was hard. Living in a tiny glass-blowing village in the middle of the woods, with few or no potential suitors, sounded as interesting to her as a life counting grains of sand, especially after nearly three years in the hustle and bustle of Grantville. "I would like to open the next 'Up-Time Bagels & Cream Cheese Café' in Saalfeld, which is not so far from Lauscha."

Neither Rachel nor Bethel were prepared for this, especially with the first café still under construction. Rachel broke the silence. "I know a Jewish family whose son Schmuel, Samuel, wants to apprentice to become a bagel baker. I had already planned to ask your approval today for him to start learning bagel baking from you. He can start immediately. The family doesn't want to move out of West Virginia County, but they would like to leave Grantville to save money. Saalfeld could be the solution for all of us. Samuel can work here for a few hours a day before school until he graduates next month. I am sure his parents would agree to move to Saalfeld since that is still in West Virginia County, but you will need more baking help. One new apprentice is just the start, and we are still busy getting this café open. How can we start another location before this one is open?"

Gisela's shoulders sagged as some of the stress melted away. "If we can arrange for my parents to meet this family, perhaps I can stay with them at first so *Mutti und Vatti* worry less. Securing a profitable business location for a bakery will certainly take several months, and I want to visit Lauscha before settling in to start a new café. I do not believe it could open before the end of summer or even the fall, at the earliest. That will give this Schmuel Samuel time to gain some skill before moving to the new location."

Bethel finally spoke. "It's a fantastic idea, but we need to look at our finances and our staff. You'll need at least one trained baker with you, preferably two journeymen, one or two apprentices, a much closer source of cream cheese, and, of course, a kosher kitchen for the bagels. Rachel seems to have a head start on solving that problem, if Schmuel's mother is willing to oversee the kitchen. There's a lot of work to do and not much time before you leave Grantville."

"Why do you think I spend all of my time at the bakery? None of our staff have been full time so I could train and hire more of them. Once we start a second location, they can all go full-time. Hopefully. I hired *and trained* three new bagel bakers, one very senior journeyman, two very junior journeyman, three apprentices, and now we have Schmuel. They were all training in the regular baker's guild before they came to Grantville. It's enough for two shops, barely, but enough to get started. We are all still learning and perfecting the craft of bagel baking, but they show promise. Plus Johan, of course. He's not officially on staff, but he is here an awful lot." She grinned and wiggled her eyebrows. "When he isn't with Krystal! Oops. I mean chaperoning his sister." They all giggled at that because it was as clear as clear could be to everyone that Sibylle spent time with Krystal so that Johan could spend time with Krystal. The only ones who couldn't quite see it were, naturally, Johan and Krystal, both of whom utterly failed to see their interest was mutual.

Rachel nodded her agreement. "If things work out with Schmuel's family, I think his mother would oversee the kitchen, and hopefully help find a local cheesemaker, if we ask her. I got the feeling his sister

Rivka might be interested in becoming an apprentice as well. *Frau* Cohen's parents ran a small butcher shop, so she has some related experience. The other side of kosher from dairy kosher, but there are a lot of similarities. You are sure your family is okay with this, Gisela? You could live with *Juden*? Truly?"`

"Yes. Jews wouldn't be their first choice, but it's a lot safer for me than living by myself. We have been in Grantville for a long time now. They do not mind *Juden* so much now. Don't forget, we need a new head baker here soon. Johan is the best candidate I know of, but of course it isn't my place to hire a head baker. If Johan doesn't want to open a bakery of his own now that he is a master baker in his own right, he'd be a real catch as head baker."

Bethel smiled beatifically. "I'll talk with Johan, reiterating how little up-timers, like my niece, care about guild status when considering becoming betrothed, and the possible financial benefits to him in being one of our first unofficial 'master bagel bakers'. Not that he is interested in being betrothed to an up-timer, of course."

"Of course," agreed Rachel and Gisela in unison, with matching giggles and grins.

"Back to the question at hand of a second location in Saalfeld. The train runs there and many people in Saalfeld have lived in or visited Grantville. We could start with a food cart at the railroad station before we jump in with a whole café. We should be able to send one of the assistant bakers, possibly one journeyman, Schmuel, and one of the other apprentices. We just need to see who might be willing to move or temporarily relocate, and what the needs are for each location. Like when we started with catering here, that lets us see if there really is demand before we spend a ton of money on a bakery and ask Schmuel's family to move there."

Rachel nodded. "*Frau* Cohen can oversee the kitchen and keep it kosher, if she's willing. She has two small daughters born since they came to Grantville, which might complicate things for her. I worry more about finding more journeymen willing to work with her and Gisela in Saalfeld than I do about finding a head baker here. Finding men who will listen to a woman boss can be quite challenging, and decent bakers are in high demand everywhere."

Bethel gave her a hard look. "And why does the baker need to be a man?"

Rachel practically stuttered her reply. "Because guild rules…. Women aren't allowed to…. Men are taught…." Her shoulders sagged. "I guess they don't, but how would that work? Will men, including young ones like Schmuel, listen to a woman as head baker? They listen in Grantville, but what happens when there is a café not in Grantville? Also, having a woman as a head baker will make the baker's guild angry. It is in West Virginia County, but it is outside Grantville."

"Let them be angry. Guilds have no standing in West Virginia County, and Saalfeld is in West Virginia County. If they won't listen to a woman, then they can't work for us. If the best person is a man, fine. If it's a woman, fine. If it's a leprechaun, fine. I draw the line at soot sprites, though. Messes follow them everywhere. Hiring them is never worth the effort. I've got your back on this, and so do all the other up-timers."

Gisela practically floated as she left. They liked the idea! They genuinely liked it! They liked her idea so much they were going to let *her* open the new store! She, Gisela Schulte, would be the head baker and boss in a real, live bakery! This was more than she had ever dared dream of back in Bohemia.

* * *

Bethel stopped short outside the kitchen door. Based on the torrent of colorful Amideutsch, Gisela's baking was not going well this morning. Hearing something slammed down on the counter and footsteps heading her way, Bethel backpedaled a few steps, then moved to the side to avoid being bowled over.

Gisela's eyes flashed as she stormed through the door, then pulled up short at the sight of Bethel. After several deep calming breaths, as recommended in the refugee housing in 1631, she started talking. "There was 'corn meal' in the cupboard and I decided to try making 'cornbread'. The recipe was on the bag. It did not end well. Everything was going fine. Then, after the cornbread was cool, I removed it from the pan and found the inside undercooked. I have enough 'corn meal' to try again, but I am angry with myself for wasting something we have so little of."

Bethel visibly relaxed and nodded. "Yeah, I get that. Anytime I use the last of anything from up-time, I stress out a bit. You should have seen me the day I used the last of my favorite lipstick. I was a mess! But I'm sure we'll get more cornmeal, and that was too old to be good anyway. My guess is that was the problem, not something you did. Cornmeal is definitely something a miller can make, as soon as we have corn to spare. We have a transplanted Texan here in town and more than a bit of Southern influence in our cooking. My guess is someone already talked to at least one miller about making cornmeal and at least a little bit is available, somewhere, or will be soon, so don't stress yourself out about it. Honestly, cornmeal fresh from the miller will almost certainly taste better than the months-old, boxed stuff we used up-time, and what you were using was *years* old. But if you have any extra of that next batch of cornbread, I won't say no to being a taste-tester! And now," Bethel took Gisela by the elbow and steered her into a nearby room, "it is time for our weekly business meeting, which is great timing since you clearly need a break from the kitchen."

Bethel sat last. "Thanks, everyone, we are all busy, so we'll get right to it. Gisela is our resident baker, and she has been experimenting with making cornbread today. We are both hoping to find fresh cornmeal *soon*. Whenever we do, we can add cornbread to our menu. Speaking of adding items, I have a request to make of both Gisela, as our baker, and Rachel, as our researcher. Cheesecake! If we can make it, cheesecake will be a high-end specialty item because of how much cream cheese and sugar the recipe needs. My recollection from high school is that baking cheesecake is a long process that requires a great deal more care than something like brownies. *But* cheesecake could make our cream cheese famous and sought after. What say you, ladies?"

Rachel spoke first. "I'm confused, but I'm in. I don't understand how cream cheese can make a cake, but if there is a recipe for cheesecake in Grantville, I'll find it!"

Gisela answered slowly. "I'm not sure either, but I am willing to try. Can you describe cheesecake?"

"It's kind of hard to describe. Cheesecake has a crust like a pie does, but not a pie crust because it's thicker and made from crushed cookies or graham crackers. The filling is thick like a pudding but ends up firm. Not soft and oozy like a pie but not like a regular cake either. You bake it low and slow for a lot more hours than either a pie or cake bake. Once you eat a slice, you'll be a fan." The more Bethel described cheesecake, the more skeptical the down-timers became, but they didn't go back on their agreement. They did mentally move cheesecake into the 'take it on faith, up-timers are weird' category.

Gisela looked back and forth from Rachel to Bethel, then simply said, "You'll need to find a recipe for these 'graham crackers' too, Rachel. Preferably before my family leaves for Lauscha next month."

CHAPTER 11

June 1634

The Schulte family stepped off the train from Grantville and looked around the Saalfeld station for their contact. Raymond had arranged for someone to pick them up and take them to a respectable inn. They had never visited Saalfeld and wanted to look around the area a bit before heading to Lauscha. "Schulte" was written on a sign held by a young man in front of the station on a neatly painted wagon in "Inn of Plenty". The entire family and their luggage fit in easily. Their household goods were following at a slightly more leisurely pace in the new horse-drawn cart Heinrich purchased the previous week.

When it became apparent that they were headed out of Saalfeld, Heinrich became suspicious. Perhaps this was not the right cart, or perhaps Raymond had been duped and this young man was part of a group of thieves or worse taking advantage of the family. Raymond didn't seem the type, but up-timers could be far too trusting. "Where are we going? Why aren't we at the Inn of Plenty yet?"

The driver acted a bit embarrassed and defiant, but not dangerous. "My name is Jeremias Ebert, and we are headed to the Inn of Plenty in Garnsdorf. I intend no harm, but I was perhaps a little not honest." Seeing their alarm, he hurried on. "Nothing bad! I hope. I only did not say that the inn is in Garnsdorf, not Saalfeld. Many people come to Saalfeld now to work for the oil company and for related projects. Many others come through to use the railroad and their number keeps growing. In Garnsdorf, we would like these people to visit our town and spend their money, their 'tourist dollars', but we have nothing of interest. The inn is new, because of the oil fields and railroad. We have up-time style plumbing and an exceptionally clean kitchen," his pride evident in every word, "but still, every night there are empty rooms because our inn is not quite so close to the railroad. People do not know we exist."

"Understood. Your town is boring and not in the center of anything. So why are we staying there?" Like her husband, Anna Maria was suspicious of Jeremias' intentions.

"Garnsdorf heard what Lauscha is planning, and that your family is going there to help them. They will be the Glass Christmas Ornament Town, but they are too far up in the hills to visit easily and traveling in the Thuringerwald is not safe. We wish to have them bring their ornaments to Garnsdorf to sell, and you can ask them for us.

"At our last town meeting, the Garnsdorf citizens decided to 'go big or go home'. We sent a petition to our Senator requesting to change our name to Kristkindlmarkt. Unlike Duke Casimir, we are told our Senator will have to take the request to the Congress and they will have to approve a name change as well. We are so proud to be part of West Virginia County now! If they agree, it will be Christmas all year in our town! *Frau* Schneider, you can teach your crafting classes. *Fraulein* Schulte, you can make your gingerbread houses. And *Herr* Schulte, you can start by helping us convince the glassmakers in Lauscha to sell their wares in our town and then sell your gingerbread molds. Garnsdorf is even willing to build the first shop for the glassmakers of Lauscha, to show our commitment. When you are at our Inn, *Mutti und Vatti* will talk to you more about the plans and ideas." With that, he turned around and they finished the drive in silence, the Schultes dumbfounded by the opportunity that had just dropped into their laps, like a heaven-sent miracle. Gisela spent most of the rest of the trip simply repeating 'thank you for the miracle, God' in her head.

"Welcome to the Inn of Plenty! I am your host, Erasmus Ebert, and my lovely wife, Dorothea Bauerin, is in the kitchen finishing your dinner. I can see from your expressions that young Jeremias explained some of what we want to talk to you about on the ride here. Please settle yourselves in the rooms at the top of the steps, to the right. The doors are open and the 'bathroom' is at the end of the hall. We have plenty of time to talk and walk around Garnsdorf after dinner. Tomorrow, Jeremias will take you back into Saalfeld, if you wish. This 'shuttle' to the train station is a service we provide for all our guests."

* * *

"*Frau* Bauerin, that meal was a revelation. I had no idea anyone outside of Grantville made quesadillas! How did you get the idea?" Heinrich's favorite Grantville food cart served quesadillas. His saddest moment in leaving Grantville wasn't knowing he wouldn't have indoor plumbing anymore; it was knowing he wouldn't have quesadillas.

"One of the workers in Saalfeld showed me. An up-timer woman and one of the millers are making a special flour for this 'Mexican' food. They said it isn't quite right yet, but we are happy with it. The tortillas and quesadillas are so easy to make, easy to carry, and easy to eat that we serve them almost every day. We also love the burritos, but I haven't figured out the tacos yet. Since no one else knows how easy they are to make, the profits are impressive." Dorothea grinned at them. "I know these aren't Christmas foods, but we are working hard to find ways to make people want to visit our little hamlet."

Initially distracted, Gisela focused in on the conversation when it turned to food. "We talked about these foods before leaving Grantville, hoping someone would make the special corn flour soon. As you can see, *Vatti* loves them. Does this miller also make 'cornmeal'?"

Dorothea's eyebrows raised almost to her hairline. "I have never heard of 'cornmeal' so I do not think so. We can ask him. Do you have a sample he can see?"

"The up-timers will need to ask around. Otherwise, Rachel has another research project. She's a researcher I know at the Grantville library. Until then, can you show me how to make these quesadillas and burritos? Perhaps we can start a cooking club here in Saalfeld!

For today, your husband said that Jeremias can take us back to Saalfeld. We want to find a location, hopefully near the train station, for a bagel café. Any interest in helping us look?"

"Perhaps, but for now, have you thought about selling your bagels and cream cheese on a food cart at the train station? We paid for much of this new inn by selling burritos and quesadillas there. Many people on the trains do not have enough time to walk even a half block to a café but will happily buy food from a cart. Erasmus and I sometimes talk about opening a restaurant in Saalfeld, but adding that expense is hard when carts are so profitable, and so much cheaper to run."

"What about building someplace on the road between Saalfeld and Garnsdorf? The restaurant could make food for the carts as well, then you store the carts inside at night. That would ensure the new restaurant becomes profitable sooner and give people a reason to walk toward Garnsdorf."

Two hours later, Dorothea had rousted down-time property manager/realtor Heironymous Cott out of his office. They were looking at the (exceedingly) few available properties near the train station and she was thinking about asking him to show them property on the road between Saalfeld on Garnsdorf.

At the third property, Anna Maria stopped cold outside the door as Dorothea was about to enter. "I will not enter. It is unsafe. My husband is a woodworker, and this wood has gone bad. It will not hold." *Herr* Cott tried to convince them, but Anna Maria eventually lost patience. "Do you think me a fool, *Herr* Cott, or an idiot? It is either one or the other, or perhaps you are the fool or idiot, because this building is not sound. I have been married to a woodworker for nearly twenty-five years and I promise you, this wood is not sound."

Faced with her intransigence, Heironymous gave in and took them to the next potential shop. This time, Dorothea gave him the evil eye. "Do not think me a fool or an idiot, either, *Herr* Cott. This shop is empty because thieves break in so often no one can earn a living here."

As they trudged back to meet Jeremias after looking at several more potential, but ultimately unsuitable, sites, Heironymous trying to convince them to lease one of the properties they had seen, Gisela finally snapped. "*Mutti und Frau* Bauerin are putting up with you, but I can't take it anymore. This is West Virginia, not some backward English shire. We can make the decisions ourselves. Stop asking for men who can 'make decisions' for us. Stop telling us things we know are wrong! Stop treating us like idiots! In fact, go away. Go back to your little office and if we need your help, we'll call you. Don't call us."

Herr Cott's chest swelled in a truly prodigious manner as he prepared to cut her down to size. Before he could speak, Dorothea did. "She's right. Go home, Heironymous, and before you start speaking, remember that I know your wife quite well. We are trying to convince these fine women and their family to live in Garnsdorf and start businesses there, in addition to a food cart or café here in Saalfeld, so you might want to go home. Now." Still huffing and beet red, Heironymous chose to bow and leave, furious to be treated that way *by women in public!*

THE GOURMETS OF GRANTVILLE

"So much for finding a property for your new café today." Dorothea put her coins on the counter of the tiny coffee shop near the train station. "This is the best coffee in Saalfeld, by the way. They get their beans straight off the train. If you do decide to go with a cart, you might consider partnering with them. You sell their coffee on your cart, and they sell your bagels in the store."

A woman poked her head out from the kitchen. Her wet apron, rolled shirt sleeves, and glistening hands and forearms said she had been washing dishes. "You want to start a food cart? What kind of food?"

Gisela noticed the woman's French accent. "Bagels and cream cheese. Mostly bagels. They are an up-time breakfast food, easy to carry in your hand."

"Ah, so what you wish to sell would indeed go well with coffee. Hans, I am taking a break now to talk to these women. The dishes can wait. Run and bring my husband here. Quickly. I will watch the shop." As the young man left, she wiped her hands on her apron, then held one out to shake. "I am Claudette Arbaleste. My husband and I are Calvinist and moved to West Virginia for the freedom of religion. We heard about the up-timer love for coffee and our congregation raised money so we could start this coffee shop. We are the first from our town, but we will help others like us move here and find jobs. I tell you this because we may be able to work together, but I must know if you have a problem with us being Calvinist."

"After three years in Grantville? Not at all." Claudette looked skeptical when Anna Maria said 'three years,' since Grantville had only been around for three years and one month. Anna Maria

185

laughed. "Fair enough, I rounded. Two years, eleven months. We were some of the first to arrive, so we were lucky enough to live in an up-time house with two genuine up-timers, both younger than my Gisela, here. Their parents were left up-time, so they needed adults in the house with them.

"Gisela is quite the baker," she gave her daughter a quick, embarrassing squeeze, "which got her a position as head baker when they started a new business baking 'bagels' and she will be the boss at this new location. So, I guess we need to know if you have a problem with thumbing your nose at the guilds?"

A short, slender man with impressive mustaches walked through the door with young Hans and gave Claudette a quick kiss. "Thumbing our nose at the guild? Any guild in particular? Happy to thumb my nose at most, overjoyed at a few."

"Glad to hear it. I'm Anna Maria. This is my daughter Gisela, a baker, and this is our new friend Dorothea from the Inn of Plenty in Garnsdorf. It may be nothing, but the bakers may become angry with us. We plan to sell bagels and cream cheese, an up-time breakfast favorite, possibly on a food cart, possibly in a shop, if we can find a space to rent. Bagels are baked, like bread, but they are an up-timer thing and very different from bread. They are chewy. It's hard to explain. You just have to eat one. Up-timers love them for breakfast. They make great sandwiches, and they do, indeed, go well with coffee, so if you know of any space nearby that we can rent, this may be the start of a promising new venture."

"Maybe. Maybe not. You can see that everything is coffee themed in here, including the walls being brown? They were white when we moved in, but this close to the train station, everything gets covered in soot. Painting the ceiling and walls coffee colored made cleaning easier. Ironically, it helped business because people have learned to look for 'the shop with coffee brown walls' when they want good coffee. We bought both sides of this building. For now, we rent out the other side. There is a small bakery there, but they run the business like it is in the middle of a market, outside. They have a cart they take to the station with their bread on display. They lose half of what they make because soot gets on it, then no one will buy it. We hear them talking through the walls and do not think they will be in business long, but they could surprise us. So, maybe, maybe not. This is a good place for selling, but not such a good place for baking."

Gisela started to answer but Dorothea spoke faster. "We will have a bakery in Garnsdorf they can use."

Gisela added her piece. "We will also have a woman, *Frau* Cohen, in charge of keeping the kitchen clean. She and her family are waiting to know that we have a place for them to live and work before they move to Saalfeld."

Claudette and Leon raised their eyebrows in unison at that. "A Jew? You really must be tolerant. I'll be honest, I'm not comfortable with that, but this is West Virginia so we will try. Are their kitchens truly as clean as people say?"

Gisela answered. "Yep. Up-timers are maniacs about clean kitchens. A lot of them choose to hire kosher cooks when they move far from Grantville because those are the only people they trust to keep a kitchen clean enough. So, we will have a clean kitchen with

Frau Cohen in charge, and, apparently, the opportunity to use a bakery in Garnsdorf, if needed."

"I cannot show you now, but if you tell me where to find you, we will ask the bakers and contact you. Perhaps they are ready to leave and try again somewhere less competitive. Truthfully, they are competent bakers, but bad at business. This is not the first bakery they have lost because they are bad businessmen. As I said, the walls are thin and we hear them talking. There is a small storeroom above the shop where they live right now. So close to the railroad, the noise in the room is very loud, but perhaps this *Frau* Cohen and her family could live there." Leon shook his head. "The lack of ghettos is still odd to me. The notion of Jews living anywhere they wish? Possibly being my neighbors and I might not even know it? Such strange ideas these up-timers are spreading."

Anna Maria had a considering look. "Hmm. Perhaps there is a better opportunity here than you realize. Competent bakers, you say? Can they work with women as bosses? If so, this may work out very well indeed. We need to find more bakers to train. They may be able continue to live there, if they wish, if we hire them. Can you talk to them? We are at The Inn of Plenty in Garnsdorf for a few days. If we aren't there, leave a message. They'll give it to us when we come back."

✳ ✳ ✳

As they traveled to Lauscha, everyone in Gisela's family was lost in their own thoughts. Heinrich broke the silence first. "I did not see that coming. Not even a little bit."

Gisela's excitement bubbled out once the silence was broken. "I can send for Margaretha! Together, we can open a shop to sell gingerbread cookies and houses. When we have made some money, perhaps we can also sell hot chocolate. There is something for all of us! Our family will be famous, and Tyrone will finally be able to court Margaretha properly."

Anna Maria was more than a little excited, too, and a little bit more than that scared. "If–*if* mind you–it happens, this could be a huge opportunity for us. We still have most of the money we have invested in OPM. They showed us a site near the center of town where we could build a shop. They don't know about the OPM money, but with that, we might be able to buy the land instead of renting."

"It is too risky. I forbid it!" That was Heinrich's first mistake.

"You *forbid* it? Do you forget who found OPM? Me. Do you forget who found us the way to earn the money in OPM by selling up-timer things for them? Agatha. Do you forget who earned more money teaching classes? Me. Do you forget who earned money selling baked goods? Gisela. Yes, you earned money in OPM too, but you were *not* the only one. So, I repeat, you *forbid* this?" When they heard Anna Maria use that tone, her children always apologized and did whatever she wanted, immediately. Her temper erupted rarely, but spectacularly. Her husband had either not learned that lesson or had forgotten it.

"Yes, I forbid it! Teaching classes to women will never make enough money to pay the bills! These gingerbread houses are nothing more than a fad, a passing fancy. This whole Christmas Town idea is foolishness, and only fools will buy into it." That was his second mistake, and Heinrich had barely finished speaking when his kind and loving wife carefully stopped the wagon, then gave him a very large push off the wagon seat, making sure he landed safely before restarting the wagon. They did not stop for him and by the time he caught up, the only place to sit was in the back, on some dirty, prickly hay, giving him plenty of time to think about his mistakes on the road to Lauscha.

June 1634

Rachel and Bethel,

When my family reached Saalfeld, a cart from the inn met us. We expected to go there to await the rest of our things while we looked around Saalfeld a bit. Instead, the driver took us out of Saalfeld entirely to a nearby small town called Garnsdorf. To make a long story short, the town heard about what Lauscha plans and has watched all the people flooding into Saalfeld. They decided to focus on getting the visitors to spend their free time (and money) in Garnsdorf by focusing the whole village on up-time style Christmas, all year. They want to sell the ornaments from Lauscha, but also have Mutti teach her craft classes and sell things she makes, and they will expand from there. They are planning a bakery, too!

I may have a chance to open a shop for the gingerbread I love to make, but that is for the future. For now, I do not have the money, and they do not have the visitors, for a shop that only sells gingerbread but, with your help, I can build a bakery there now to bake the bagels and cheesecakes. Then, I can start making cookies and gingerbread when the time is right. Baking them right in the store is better, but the best place to start selling them is near the train station and the air is too dirty there. A kitchen would never stay clean enough. In a year or two, when you can find a better location, I can buy the bakery in Garnsdorf (or whatever they change the name to, since they plan to change the name) from you and start baking whatever I can earn a living from. The town enthusiastically supports my opening a bakery here, if I bake cookies and gingerbread, not just bread. I love not having guilds!

Mutti and a woman from Garnsdorf visited Saalfeld with me to find a location for the cafe. We found a storefront near the station that everyone agreed should work. We are waiting to hear if the people renting it are staying or going. We were told they are competent bakers but bad at business. If true, we might have the new bakers we need for the shop. Hoping that you like this plan, I used part of my small savings to hold the storefront for a few weeks. If you don't like it, we have lost relatively little. I'm enclosing a small map, in case you have time and want to see the space. The owners of the coffee shop marked on the map can help you since they own the building. The best way to find them is to 'ask for the shop with the coffee brown walls'.

Please write back and tell me what you think of this plan. We are going to visit Lauscha tomorrow to find out if they agree to their part of this plan, but you can send a note to the Inn of Plenty in Garnsdorf and I will get it when I return. They have your names.
- Gisela

Saalfeld, West Virginia County

"It's perfect!" Bethel didn't realize how nervous she had been until she felt her stress melt away. Two short blocks from the train station, but next to the tracks, the bakery café had space to store a small food cart, a direct path to the station, and, of course, a coffee shop next door. Whenever a train arrived, they could be at the station quickly to sell to hungry travelers. The small front counter was serviceable. The living space above could be used to expand the store with a small space to allow someone to live on-site for security, if the current bakers moved out. The place was reasonably clean, aside from the inevitable soot, but the kitchen was too small for much baking even without the soot issue. After ten minutes, they had examined every inch and were ready for a quick trip to Garnsdorf, mostly to time the trip from potential bakery to storefront.

"I'd like the bakery to be closer, but if we have a well-insulated cart to keep the bagels fresh, warm, and clean, this might do well enough. Realistically, most people will have never eaten a bagel, so they won't know how much better they are warm, so a cart should be fine. I'm less sure about the storefront. I want to hear your thoughts, Rachel." Rachel often hid her thoughts and opinions, expecting older (and non-Jewish) people to want her to stay silent. Bethel encouraged her to speak her mind on something beyond research and recipes, but it was slow going.

"That's hard. The air is too dirty for a café, but the location is convenient to the train station. It's too small to serve many people, but we can't bake much there anyway. I guess this isn't a bad place to start, but we need to find somewhere bigger, and cleaner, to start a real café. Maybe we keep this location to feed people on the train and open a storefront someplace else in town once people here start to want bagels? Maybe we only keep it for the six months we can pay for right now and then move entirely to another location? I don't know about you, but I don't feel like you can make that decision yet." Rachel seemed to be confident in her thoughts, but less confident in how well they would be received. Her voice was decidedly tentative.

"What about the bakers?"

"The food was decent. The service wasn't awful, but it was slow and I saw them make mistakes with other customers. They don't seem to know where to find anything customers need. If they covered the bread, they wouldn't have as much spoilage from soot. The rolls were the best I've had since…. I guess they're just the best I've ever had. So, they are bakers with some skill in a decent location but losing their shirts because they have bad business practices, like letting soot settle all over the food. If they can't keep their business and we have someone else managing the place, Gisela is right. We should ask them if they want to train with her. But I don't know about them living here. There isn't much space, and they should be closer to the bakery. What do you think about having the person who manages the business live here instead of the baker?"

"That's the start a solid plan and I agree with all of it. Let's go with that as *our* initial plan. Trust yourself more! You're really getting this. You and your family own a solid chunk of this business. It's not only mine, and it's definitely not my husband's. We own it together, you and me. Please send a note back to Garnsdorf for Gisela outlining what we just decided while we wait for the next train back. The young man with the shuttle to the inn can take it for us. After you send that, we can look around town a little. Once she gets back from Lauscha, Gisela can open the new bakery and the shop, find a new location for the café, buy the supplies we need, and train the new employees." After listing everything Gisela needed to do, Bethel started looking thoughtful.

Rachel spoke first. "I think we are both realizing this is perhaps too much work for Gisela to do herself. I will talk to my family and move to Saalfeld to help her open the café. This will also give me more experience to help others with opening new locations. I have read in the library about up-time 'franchises' that gave extraordinarily specific directions to restaurants, so your experience was the same every time you went into a McDonalds, Subway, or whatever restaurant. We can try to copy this plan, so they are at least similar. Will you be okay with that?" Rachel was excited thinking about all the possibilities!

Seeing Bethel's anxiety rising as she spoke, Rachel hurried to reassure her. "I don't mean move permanently! Just for a month or two. I will be back in Grantville helping you before Channukah, and I will stay there until after the grand opening of the café. Your Christmas time. I truly, truly, *truly* appreciate your central heating in the winter!" This got a grin and a hug from Bethel, on board with the newly modified plan.

July 1634

The morning of the day of the grand opening, Bethel arrived at the Grantville café shortly after Gisela delivered their custom order from her. "Gisela, it's fantastic. I don't know how you did it, but you captured the building perfectly. With all the detail that went into this, making it must have taken you forever. I'm speechless."

Rachel glanced at her. "For someone who is 'speechless', you are talking a lot, but I agree with *Frau* Little. When you said you would build a model of our shop in gingerbread, I did not truly believe any gingerbread house could be worthy of our new shop, but this is magnificent. Where did you find the molds to make it, or do you hand-carve the design?"

Gisela paused before answering. "It's a trade secret, but I can make quite a bit of custom detail. If anyone asks, my dad made the gingerbread molds."

Bethel groused at Rachel, "I told you to call me Bethel. We are business partners! You make me uncomfortable calling me *Frau* Little all the time, like we barely know each other. Also, Gisela, I talked to the reporter who will be covering the grand opening for *The Grantville Times*, Betsy Springer, and she agreed to do a piece on your work."

"Truly? A newspaper article on me? Why? When?"

"It may not run this week, but your business should get a nice boost when it does. Not to put too fine a point on it, but she's going to talk to you during the grand opening celebration, which starts in two hours, to learn more about gingerbread houses and your fledgling business. You might want to run home and freshen up a bit."

"Right. Sorry, Bethel. I'll go home and clean up, so I look respectable and try to think of some things to say. I'll see if I can find any history on gingerbread houses between now and then. I doubt it, in such short time, but I need to at least try. See you later!"

As the door swung shut behind Gisela, Rachel spoke. "Everything is set here. The bakers need to bake, and we need the delivery of cream cheese, neither of which needs me. Otherwise, we're ready to go. I know Gisela spent a lot of time on that gingerbread model and we didn't pay her much. I'm going to run over to the library and do an hour or so of research for her. I'm still on the lists as a researcher, after all. I might as well make myself useful!"

* * *

A few hours later, they had a list of customers for the next batch of cream cheese and a line of customers waiting for the next batch of bagels to be ready. Betsy had enough material for three articles, one on the bagel bakery, one on gingerbread houses, and one on the different cheeses available from The Cow Barnes. She also had an idea for a Christmas story for *The Grantville Inquisitor*. Lyle would be pleased.

Heinrich started getting requests for custom gingerbread molds mailed to him in Garnsdorf the next day. Except for having one of the door handles break off one of the precious up-time ovens, everything went better than they had expected.

* * *

"Heinrich! Anna Maria! We did not expect you back so soon. I hope this means Lauscha likes the idea?"

"Indeed they do, Erasmus. They have decided to not to change their name since Garnsdorf wants a Christmas name. Truth to tell, I think they were having second thoughts about how easy getting approval would be, even for such a new town. They are still talking about the details and a lot of bigger plans, but they were firmly in favor of them making the ornaments and Garnsdorf, under whatever the new name is, selling them. Our family decided to come back early to have the first pick of available lots. If Garnsdorf is amenable, we will start building our home and business this summer, so we can be warm and snug before winter."

Erasmus and Dorothea beamed as if they had just gotten the brass ring on the Merry Go Round. "Of course! Let us look at the land and talk specifics. Now that you have talked with the people in Lauscha and had time to think over our idea for a few days, we will gather the town and talk over our plans with you. You have seen the up-timers Christmas, perhaps you have some ideas to share with us?"

Young Dietrich piped up. "I think you should be the Burgermeister! That's the name they use in the up-time Christmas movie about Santa, and I like it! You can be the Burgermeister Meisterburger, and Gisela can be the Bäckermeister Meisterbäcker. *Vatti* can be the Baumeister Meisterbau and…."

"Enough, Dietrich! We get the idea. Now, stop being silly and go find some kids and play for a bit. You will need to unload our things soon so don't go far." Anna Maria was more amused than annoyed, but Dietrich was a chatterbox and they had business to attend to. "Baumeister Meisterbau indeed. Silly boy."

Erasmus looked amused at the silliness. "Jeremias did those kind of silly rhyming names when he was little. Using those silly names would be tempting, to amuse the children, if it didn't saddle us with such long titles. Perhaps we shall use up-time titles. 'Mayor' is so much shorter than 'Burgermeister', but that's a decision for another day.

"We have been reading about up-time Christmas. Almost all of us have visited Grantville at Christmas for a day or so. Up-time Christmas is different than regular Christmas. Bigger. Snowier. More decorations. Because the Santa Claus is important to up-time Christmas, we wish to have a home and workshop for him on our town square. Up-time, they took photos of their children with the Santa. Dogs as well, for some reason. For our version, our idea is to make copies of this drawing of Santa," Erasmus held up one sheet from a stack that showed Santa sitting in his sleigh with an opening beside him, "and draw each child on the seat beside him. An artist will finish the drawing while the family waits. This sketch will be a nice memento, the kind of thing one shares with friends and family, and there are always decent artists willing to work cheap.

"We want the bakeshop and a cocoa shop next door to Santa's house, across from the workshop. Santa loves cookies, cocoa, and milk." Erasmus shuddered a bit. "Why anyone old enough to walk would drink cow milk on purpose is beyond me, so we are down-playing that part. At any rate, the woodworking and craft stores will be a little further down the street, past the Lauscha ornament shop. There will also be a store with dolls across the street. They are rare, but we are hoping to find a doll maker to move here, although that may take a few years. With you being one of the first to agree to move here, and with such clear Christmas goods to sell, you will have many excellent choices for your bakeshop and other endeavors."

Gisela noted his odd phrasing. "Why do you say 'bakeshop' instead of 'bakery'?"

"We have big plans! Big plans, indeed. Our dream is that our Christmas town will grow so large that the cookie shop next to Santa will need so much space for cookies and gingerbread that there will be no space for a kitchen. The goods will need to be baked in a second location. A lot has already been reserved for the bakery. A second street is planned street behind the shops, including the bakeshop and Santa's workshop. One street behind each set of shops, for three streets running through town, to start. The bakery, woodshop, and other craft workshops will be there to support the storefronts selling their goods. Families may also have their workers live over their workshops while they live over the store, or the other way around. Places like the blacksmith that generate a lot of noise and dirt will be a bit farther away, but they may also have space for their workers to live near the shops. Goods will only need to be walked across the back street." Erasmus beamed as if he had just won Grand Prize at the County Fair with a last-minute entry. He thought the plan (his, naturally) was brilliant.

They continued walking for five minutes when Erasmus stopped and gestured around a small meadow a bit south of where two paths intersected. "This will be our new town square. Closer to the roads, we will have a proper market square, later. We do not want carts and such running through the middle of Santa's workshop! They should run behind it, where the stables will be. We are also hoping to have a regular pick-up for the train station and a few places in Saalfeld but negotiations! So much comes down to negotiations. It's all so exciting." Erasmus rubbed his hands together in delight. In his heart of hearts, he was born to haggle.

Anna Maria spoke to Dorothea. "Why didn't you put the square closer to your inn, or your inn closer to the square?"

"Quiet. We wish for our Inn of Plenty to be quiet and restful for our guests. We are still close, but the business noises won't wake our guests before sunrise. We hope to open a second location quite near the square for a different clientele." Sigh. "One with small children who are noisy, if I'm honest. They can spy on Santa's workshop through windows between the inn and his workshop while *Mutti und Vatti* relax with a beer and some up-time pretzels, assuming we can find some."

Gisela perked up at the baking challenge. "On it! Soft or hard pretzels?" Erasmus looked at Dorothea, who was looking at him, both clearly uncertain. "Never mind. I'll make both. The location for the gingerbread shop, I mean bakeshop, is great, amazing in fact, but if things go well, I will need a second location just for gingerbread houses. Those are an up-time Christmas tradition. *Vatti* makes gingerbread molds, by the way. I love that there is already a space for a larger bakery. Just to remind you: at first, we want to make bagels here to sell at the train station. We will get a bakery for the bagels in Saalfeld, but you know how it is there. Finding a location is hard, and finding a *good* location is almost impossible. The one we found near the train station is okay, but small, and so sooty."

Dorothea perked up. "That's what we'll tell people to convince them to come to our town! 'Finding a room in Saalfeld is hard. Finding a good one is almost impossible. Stay in Christmas Town!' Hmm. What do you think of Christmas Town as the new name? I heard rumors that other cities and towns are going to object if we try to name ourselves Kristkindlmarkt, since most places have at least a small one."

Anna Maria answered. "That's too wordy for a motto or marketing. An up-time name gives a better flavor of what you want to do, so I think Christmas Town is a lot better than Kristkindlmarkt."

Gisela was focused. "Since we desperately need a bakery for *Up-Time Bagels & Cream Cheese*, are you okay with building out the bakery before the bakeshop? The bakery is more important to us than the shop. Your inn can sell up-time bagels for breakfast. The only other place doing that right now is the Higgins Hotel in Grantville." Dorothea's whole expression dropped and her eyes went wide when Gisela said that. "Oh no! Is that a problem, Dorothea?"

"A problem? *Mein Gott, nein!* I am thinking of how to promote that we are like the Higgins. This is like manna from heaven for our inn! As you said, we can work together and make the tortilla for the burritos and quesadillas in the bakery. Then people will start to look for the Inn of Plenty." Birds of a feather, Gisela, Anna Maria, and Dorothea started brainstorming in earnest. By the time Heinrich and Erasmus finished discussing building plans and a possible layout for the town layout, Gisela, Anna Maria, and Dorothea were hard at work on marketing plans for the Inn of Plenty and Christmas Town.

* * *

Anna Maria and Jeremias were waiting to take Dorothea back to the Inn. Since the schoolteacher in Garnsdorf had married and moved away, they needed a new one. As she walked up, her body language radiated fury. Dorothea was spitting nails. "Those pestiferous, punctilious, pencil-pushing pansies! They won't even face me. They are hiding behind their 'rules', telling me we can't have a new school for Garnsdorf! *We're already building the school ourselves!* But no, we can't open the school we are building because they don't have a teacher to give us, and there are new rules about who can be a teacher. Training they need. Sure, you can keep teaching if you've already been doing it for years, but new teachers? They must have *training*. Teacher training. And how do they get it? Go to Grantville. Grantville, where it's expensive to live. Grantville, where there is no housing to rent even if you have the money. Grantville, where the classes are all full even if you find a place to live! Always, these bureaucrats," the venom in her voice was impressive, "tell us to go to another town for another form, an approval, a piece of paper telling them that some other bureaucrat approves of us doing something everyone already knows we are perfectly capable of doing!

"How are our children supposed to learn? Our last teacher got married and moved. It's a long walk to the next closest school. For generations, we have found our own teachers and our children have learned from them, now they say we aren't able to do that. They need the forms saying the teachers are good enough! What do they want us to do? How do we find one of these magical trained teachers and convince them to move here? Or one who's been teaching for years and can still teach? If we don't, where do we send the children? Do they just not go to school?" Dorothea looked ready to continue for hours.

Anna Maria cleared her throat. "I, ah, might, perhaps, be able to help with your problem."

Dorothea looked at her disbelievingly. "You know an up-time trained teacher looking for work, here, in Garnsdorf?"

"In a manner of speaking. You know I teach what they call crafting classes? The woman who pushed me to start doing that, *Frau* Flannery, also convinced me to take the teacher training classes at the vo-tech so I could do a better job teaching crafts. I am trained as an up-time style teacher. Since I need to train others to teach the crafting classes, I also became a teacher of teachers. As much as I wish they would, the craft classes won't start earning me much money this year. I can teach the children, and perhaps on weekends I can teach the teachers, so they are trained up-time style teachers, as well. Next year, we may have enough up-time trained teachers for an up-time style elementary school."

That took the wind out of Dorothea's sails, so to speak. She just said, "Huh. Did not see that coming. I'll talk to the pencil-pushers. You have the proof? All the papers and certificates the pencil-pushers will demand?"

"A certificate for teaching, plus another one for teaching teachers."

"Wait a minute. The pestiferous pencil-pushers said teacher training takes two years, but you said you could train teachers in one year."

"It is two years for a *new* teacher to learn. Experienced teachers can finish the program in one year, which the pencil-pusher may never have been told. But that is with classes every day and not teaching. If I train them, they would still be teaching during the day. Then they would be students for two or two and a half days in the weekend, plus holidays and in the summer. They should expect no time off from start to finish, except Christmas. But next year, at the beginning of the '35-'36 school year, Garnsdorf could have an entire elementary school with all the teachers trained to be up-time style teachers. We could have the first real down-time, up-time school, so we could help figure out how to combine the two kinds of schooling. Up-timers are foolish in their refusal to have kids memorize much, but we are equally foolish to not have them learn to 'debate', even the ones who are not staying in school many years."

Dorothea was pleased to hear Anna Maria saying 'we' about Garnsdorf. "Huh. Works for me. Just think of that. The first entire up-time style elementary school outside of Grantville here in Garnsdorf!" She grinned spitefully. "Sundremda can't top that." Anna Maria wasn't sure why Dorothea felt so competitive with Sundremda, but she definitely did. This wasn't the first, or last, comment like that she heard from her.

CHAPTER 12

August 1634

"Caroline, I decided we should make a special treat for Princess Kristina using our cream cheese, but this needs to be kept a surprise in case it doesn't turn out, and we need some help getting her treat to her." Bethel was being mysterious. "I need someone who can make sure her surprise stays cool, isn't jostled too much, and gets to the Princess after she finishes her growing food at lunchtime."

"I'm intrigued. Tell me more." The thoughts of Caroline, principal lady in waiting to Princess Kristina, raced along the lines of easily melted treats like buckeyes, ice cream cakes, and popsicles, momentarily detouring to chocolate chip cookies.

"Cheesecake!" Caroline's yip of glee was all the proof Bethel needed that bringing back cheesecake was indeed a grand idea. "Fingers crossed that Rachel, our resident researcher, finds a recipe for graham crackers for the crust soon. If she doesn't, we'll have to make a shortbread crust instead."

"I have to run, but make sure to tell me when you have that cheesecake. I don't want to miss the world's first cheesecake! And I don't care if you make other 'test' cheesecakes first. Officially, Princess Kristina Vasa will receive the first down-time cheesecake, and don't let your marketing department forget it!" Caroline hummed as she left, anticipating the first-ever cheesecake and how a certain young princess would react.

September 1634 Garnsdorf, SoTF

"I have good news and bad news. Which do you want first?" Bethel walked into the first business meeting of *Up-Time Bagels & Cream Cheese* in Garnsdorf.

Rachel answered before Gisela had a chance. "The bad."

"Princess Kristina loved the cheesecake. Before you ask, that's also the good news." Rachel and Gisela gave Bethel questioning looks, a bit confused by what she was saying. "She's telling everyone how much she loved the cheesecake, so a ton of people ordered cheesecakes. A bunch backed out when they found out how expensive they are, but that still leaves at least a dozen cheesecakes to make, mostly up-timers, and we aren't set up to bake and sell them in volume yet.

"Getting our Grantville location was blind luck, you must remember that, given how many places our realtor showed us before Raymond and I remembered the old lunch counter and renovated it. There's no way we're finding a place in Grantville with enough space to add a full bakery, then tie up some of the ovens for half a day at a time baking cheesecakes. We still don't have a full facility here. Since cheesecake doesn't travel terribly well, especially in hot weather, that limits us too, badly. We had to make them in home ec one year. Mine was a total failure, but it taught me that cheesecakes are finicky. I don't think we're ready to try to make them in a down-time oven just yet."

Gisela spoke after a few minutes, startling them since they had forgotten she was there. "I will help you find places to bake them, and I will help you find a way to bake them in down-time ovens. When you stop selling bagels in the afternoon, you will start selling the cheesecakes and other up-time delicacies, when you choose them, until going home at 5:00. Pre-orders only for cheesecakes. This will work. But do not forget that you need to make the 'graham crackers' for the crusts, too."

"The graham crackers! I never remember the durn graham crackers. Can you find anyone in or near Grantville to bake them? Out of their homes is fine. They can bring them to us every few days until they are able to bake the cheesecakes for us, unless you have a better idea."

Rachel answered. "I think that will work for now, but my family is discussing other places we can open cafés. They tell me the local bakers' guilds are making unhappy noises about what we are doing, but guilds are always making unhappy noises about something. Having non-guild women baking these crackers for us will only make the noises worse, even though guilds aren't allowed to operate in Grantville or Saalfeld. *Frau* Little von Up-Time, you must speak to the other up-timers so you have an answer ready when we need one. The guild masters will not listen to me or Gisela. They may not listen to you, but the ones who work most with Grantville will listen to a woman the best. Even the most backwards, hide-bound guild master has dealt with a noble woman or two he had no choice but to listen to." Bethel knew Rachel was serious since she had pulled out the "*Frau* Little von Up-Time" nonsense.

Bethel's head sank to her chest for a moment before it popped back up and she sat up straight. "Got it. One tussle with a baker's guild that doesn't exist in Grantville, and is different in every town, on the radar. I think we have a solid argument since both bagels and graham crackers were created *way* later then the seventeenth century, but there's reality and then there's politics. Even I know that much!" After a ripple of laughter, they dug into the real business of the meeting, including what staff Gisela had, what she needed, and touring the new Saalfeld and Garnsdorf locations. The Garnsdorf bakery was definitely a work in progress. The goal was to have the exterior done before winter arrived. Thanks to some local masons who loved Gisela's baking, the ovens were nearly complete. Since they were putting living space for the workers, which included the family right now, upstairs, they would have a cozy new home for the winter.

October 1634

On her forty-first birthday, Bethel walked into her boss's office and took a seat across from him. "This is it. My last few hours as a tax-collector."

"I hoped you would change your mind. Is your bagel business really doing that well?"

"It really is. We have two locations now. I never loved being a tax collector, but at the bakery, we are bringing back all kinds of things from up-time. We have been working on a new kind of cheesecake for the past few weeks. I brought one in to share with everyone to celebrate my last day, but you'll have to take a break right now to enjoy a slice."

"Ma'am, I am just a lowly gubmint toiler, who cannot afford the luxury of cheesecake, so I will be on your heels walking to wherever this confection awaits. But please, tell me you did not make pumpkin spice cheesecake." His hangdog expression at the words "pumpkin spice" made her burst into laughter.

"Pinky promise!" She glanced around, then motioned him closed. "I also promise not to knowingly bring 'pumpkin spice' back into the world. The cheesecake is caramel swirl!" Hearing those words, her very-nearly-former boss started shooing her out the door, practically drooling at the thought.

Saalfeld

Thanks to lots of elbow grease and hard work, the Saalfeld location was no longer simply a counter in a sooty, drafty space. Before the first cold days of autumn, their Lauscha connections had made new glass windows for them. They paid a reduced rate in exchange for a sign on each side of the building proclaiming where the windows had been made (the larger one visible from passing trains), and Heinrich had added a solid door with no drafts around it. Lauscha planned to specialize in glass Christmas ornaments, but they wanted snug windows for their own homes and businesses, so they were developing some skill at it. Christmas ornaments might make them famous, but good glass windows would pay the bills until that happened.

Cleaning the shop was still a never-ending chore, but it was no longer an impossible one. *Frau* Cohen was much happier and customers flocked in for the warmth, especially after they knocked an opening in the wall to pass coffee and bagels back and forth with the coffee shop. One stop for both! Win-win. Since the bagel shop had superior windows that kept it warmer and a compact room upstairs for businesses meetings, it did more business than the coffee shop. Thanks to all those additional sales, the coffee shop was nearly forty percent more profitable. Claudette and Leon had sent word for a few more people from their church to move to Saalfeld and were on the waiting list for new windows. They had seen the plans for Garnsdorf and planned on encouraging the newcomers from their church to settle there and open businesses, starting with a coffee and hot chocolate shop, initial emphasis on the coffee.

* * *

Johan hopped off the train and started looking for the bagel cart. "Excuse me young man, but I understand you have a café nearby. Where might I find it?" The young man gave Johan directions and he started on his way, noting all the other carts jostling for position around the station. In addition to food and drinks, they sold small, inexpensive items such as Dr. Gribbleflotz's cures and the latest fad, postcards of the local area.

"Johan! It's great to see you! This is a surprise. What brings you to Saalfeld?" Gisela was genuinely pleased to be visited by a friend from Grantville.

"That's going to be a bit of a longer conversation than you have time for now, judging by that line out the door, but I can stay for a day or two, so there's no rush. If I can leave my bag here, I'll wander around Saalfeld for a bit, or I can jump in and help you."

"Hmm. Go wander around. If you want to help clean up, be back in two hours. If you don't want to help clean up, three."

"Three hours it is!" Johan looked relaxed. "This is a bit of a mini 'vacation' for me. I've never been to Saalfeld before, so I'm going to try to enjoy looking around."

Garnsdorf

"Spill, Johan. What is this secret reason you are visiting me here? I know it isn't romantic because we all know you and Krystal are going to be betrothed when you get your nerve up. Don't look at me like that. You and Krystal are the only ones still tiptoeing around the matter. Do not try to change the subject. Why are you here?"

"Gisela, what was your dearest dream when you lived in Bohemia?"

Gisela tensed up and answered testily. "I told you already. To become a master gingerbread baker, which the guilds will never allow. Since there are no guilds in Grantville or anywhere else in West Virginia County, I cannot become a master here, either. Are you trying to put me in a bad mood as payback for my teasing you about Krystal?"

Johan waved his hands, as if to make that disappear. "No, no. Think about it. The things we are making, the two of us, bagels, croissants, cornbread, these are things no one in any bakers' guild is making. Bethel knows your desire to be a master baker, and everyone knows that guilds do not allow women to be masters or to own their own shops. And everyone who knows up-timers knows how much they hate that."

Gisela did not look one whit less irritated. "And? So what? Are you here to remind me what I can't do and how stupid my dream was?"

Now Johan was getting irritated. He took a deep breath and started again. "No. I am trying to explain. The up-timers, especially *Frau und Herr* Little, want us to start an up-timer bakers guild. This location seems to be doing well so they have suggested starting a third location somewhere outside of West Virginia County, but not far outside, so we can start an 'up-timer baking' guild. We set the rules, and the rules will specifically allow women to be masters and to own shops. You can be a master!"

Gisela looked gobsmacked. "Me, a master? A real master?" After a few minutes, she straightened up. "I can't think of a single reason not to. Let's do it! What do we need to do to get started, other than choosing a town?"

Saalfeld

Jost Erhardt, tinsmith, stopped at Joe's Joe near the Saalfeld train station. "Your walls really are the color of coffee. I'll take a cup of Joe, Joe."

"Do you want a bagel with that?"

"Well, yeah, but the line's too long next door."

"We have a deal with them. Order from us and they hand your bagel to us through that window right there, just like we send coffee over to their customers. Do you want your bagel with or without cream cheese?"

"With. Definitely with, but that's too expensive for me, so I'll take it with butter."

Jost walked back to the train station to watch the trains and the people while he ate. A young man already sitting there struck up a conversation with him. "What are you doing here? Day trip or something longer?"

"I'm a master tinsmith but Grantville is a bit too expensive to start a smithy, so I'm looking around to try to find someplace I can afford."

"What do you make?"

"Is this 'twenty questions'? Tell me something about yourself."

"I live in Garnsdorf. My family owns The Inn of Plenty and I drive a shuttle between there and here. When I can take a break, I like to watch the trains and talk to people. It's amazing how many different people come through here. So, what do you make, Mr. Tinsmith?"

"Cookie cutters. It's an up-time thing. Visitors buy most of them. Also, I own part of a company that makes sock knitters."

"*Mutti* loves her sock knitter! I think I've seen some of these cookie cutters. We have a baker from Grantville living in Garnsdorf now and she has some of them. What are yours shaped like? She has one they tell us is a 'cactus' that just looks weird to me. I like the gingerbread men and trees the best."

"My biggest seller is an outline of the high school. The next biggest is an outline of Julie Sims' fabled rifle. The third biggest is a small, jagged ring representing the ring of fire, perfect for use on decorative pie crusts. They make great souvenirs and gifts. The tourists love 'em, but I don't make enough money that way to build my own shop. The up-timers all think cookie cutters are too seasonal for a business and won't loan me money for a smithy. Down-timers don't understand what they do and won't loan me money."

This caught Jeremias' attention. "What season?"

"Christmas."

"We just may be able to help each other out. Are you willing to take a trip to Garnsdorf? It's not far and I'll bring you back this afternoon. There's a train about to arrive and I'll head back to Garnsdorf as soon as it departs the station again." Thirty minutes later, Jeremias had a family and their luggage securely bundled into the shuttle, and Jost and Gisela were hitching a ride in the back.

"*Fraulein*, do you work for the inn that you are riding in the back like this?"

"Goodness, no! I work at the bagel café, and I'm headed home. My family lives in Garnsdorf now, so whenever Jeremias can give me a ride, he does."

"Ah, baker's hours. Going to work is usually safer for bakers than for anyone else, because no one else is awake when you leave for work."

Gisela laughed. "I never thought of it that way, but you are right! I do feel safer walking about before work than at any other time of the day. What do you do?"

"I am a tinsmith. Jeremias said I must see Garnsdorf because he thinks there may be an opportunity there for me. I wish to start my own forge, but Grantville is too expensive. Saalfeld is also too expensive, and the things I make would not sell well there."

"What do you make?" Gisela thought of a tinsmith as someone who could make a living almost anywhere.

"Do you know what a 'cookie cutter' is?" Gisela nodded. "I make them."

"I bake cookies, especially gingerbread cookies, and I make gingerbread houses."

"That's you? I saw the one at the church last Christmas. It was amazing." A lightbulb seemed to go off in Jost's head. "Aren't you Agatha's sister?" Gisela nodded. "I'm her business partner Jost. It's a pleasure to finally meet you."

By the time they arrived at Garnsdorf, they looked like long-time friends. Gisela's parents saw them walk up to the front of the Inn of Plenty, then stand there talking until Jeremias was ready to give Jost a tour. "Husband, I think you need to be prepared for a request to court our eldest daughter. Not Agatha after all."

"Wife, I believe you are correct, and we both knew Jost and Agatha were never going to talk about anything more personal than sales figures and income statements months ago. I wonder how long until one or the other of them figures it out?"

"I just hope they don't take years. I don't have that much patience."

"*Ja,* that could take years if we don't help them along. Just look at Johan and Krystal. He moved to Grantville and still, she is unsure of his interest. Going back to Jost and Gisela, I was wondering how long until one of them figures out that he is in business with her sister." They both considered the potential couple while they talked, completely unaware of anything except each other, for a several minutes.

"Perhaps they already have, Heinrich."

"Perhaps. I hope Jost has the means to support her. The sock knitters are a nice income, but starting a smithy is expensive and someone can copy the sock knitter. He cannot rely on just that for income. It is enough for courting, but not enough for betrothal. As much as I like him, I don't know Jost well enough yet to be sure of his business sense. They both need to focus on their businesses for several years." Anna Maria couldn't have said it better herself, so she simply nodded her agreement with Heinrich.

CHAPTER 13

November 1634 Grantville

Linda sat in the choir room, already wearing her robe, waiting for the choir to arrive. Normally they would be gabbing and making lots of noise, but they knew this recital, each piece of music, was for Linda's daughter. It was impossible to miss how close Tina was to the end. Once a substantial young woman, she had wasted away over the years since the Ring of Fire into a slip of a thing, easily carried by her father, brother, or husband. Today, the choir entered quietly, stowed their personal items, donned their robes, and sat quietly, waiting.

Looking at the clock, Linda bowed her head, breathed deeply, then stood. "It is time. Is everyone ready?" Seeing nods all around, she led them in warming up their voices, then up the stairs to the choir loft.

Father Gus processed to the front of the sanctuary, genuflected, then turned and blessed the congregants. More of an audience in this case. "My children, it has been several years now since the Ring of Fire changed our world, and sometimes our hearts and minds. I like

217

to believe that it added blessings to our world, but we cannot deny that it also takes from it. Almost all the music we will hear tonight is from composers who have been taken from us, butterflied from our future. But through the miracle that God created, we still have some of their music.

"Oftentimes when we go to a musical recital, the music is chosen to represent a time, a theme, a rich patron, or a composer. Tonight's music has no such thread. It is simply the music most beloved by our own organist here at St. Mary's, Linda Bartolli, and her family. We invited Linda to speak, but she declined, asking only that we tell you that recordings of this will be available through Trommler Records with all the proceeds from them going to Leahy to fund housing for families visiting with sick patients. She calls them 'Ronald McDonald houses', although they are neither Scottish nor houses. Please enjoy the music."

When Father Gus sat, Linda moved to the piano. "Sunrise, sunset. Sunrise, sunset, swiftly flow the years…." By the end of the second line, there was no sound except the music. By the end of the second verse, tears were flowing, by the end of the song, there wasn't a dry eye in the church. Most of the up-timers knew the piece well enough to recognize that much of the song had been rewritten, although not well enough to remember the old lyrics. The changes only increased the emotional gut-punch. In later years, gentiles would be shocked to find that the song they sang at funerals and memorials was originally written about an arranged Jewish marriage. Jews, on the other hand, learned the original lyrics soon after Trommler released the recording.

Now the choir understood why their first piece was *My Favorite Things*. The shift in tempo would help them regain their composure to sing the remaining pieces, and the congregants to enjoy the music. Linda moved back to the organ for *Ave Maria*, followed by *Ode to Joy, Whither Thou Goest, Jesu Joy of Man's Desiring,* the *Hallelujah Chorus, Let Us Break Bread Together,* and *This Little Light of Mine.*

The choir's robes rustled as they sat, hands in their laps. Some sought out their own families with their eyes, others watched Linda at the organ, and a few looked to Father Gus. As the sounds from the choir quieted, the congregants noticed their stillness and quieted further themselves. When Linda started playing again, you could have heard a pin drop. The first chords from Charles-Marie Widor's *Symphony No. 5 in F Minor* were stirring in even the most mundane times. This time, they made the hair stand up on the back of the listeners necks. Linda, run-of-the-mill small town church organist, gave the performance of her life that day. No one knew it that day, but Linda would never again play that song in public. *Te Deum.* Handel's *Water Music: Suite No. 2.* Clarke's *Trumpet Voluntary.* Keys' *Arrival of the Queen of Sheba.* Clarke's *The Prince of Denmark's March.* Rawsthorne's *Hornpipe Humoresque.* Brahms' *21 Hungarian Dances.* Mouret's *Rondeau,* more commonly known to up-timers as the theme from *Masterpiece Theater.* Linda moved to the piano for her final two pieces and began playing Beethoven's *Moonlight Sonata.*

As the notes of the final piece listed in program, Scott Joplin's *Maple Leaf Rag,* faded away, the choir left the choir loft for the final song. They fanned out around the entire sanctuary, many motioning for children and grandchildren join them. Linda played the tune through once on the piano. It was easy to see which up-timers had attended Vacation Bible School or sent their kids: they looked confused as they listened to the music, sure they couldn't be hearing what they thought they were hearing, but they were. This song simply wasn't played at a serious recital. As the choir started singing a cappella, Linda motioned for the congregation to stand and moved to be with her family.

Father Abraham had seven sons. Seven sons had Father Abraham.

The very last song was Vacation Bible School (VBS) standard *Father Abraham*, complete with motions. Every summer after VBS, Tina and all the other kids would come home singing that stupid, stupid earworm, getting it stuck in everyone's heads, and doing all the motions, as best they could remember them. *Father Abraham* was a cheery, silly end to the program. Father Gus (or, more likely, his wife Hannelore), and every other pastor and priest in the area, now had a great promotional tool for VBS, but for Linda, the real joy was watching her daughter doing the motions with everyone else.

December 1634

"Over the last three years, the Grantville Cooking Club has shared many holiday favorites from up-time and down-time alike. This year, we're tackling stuffing. Stuffing is a fantastic dish because you can use whatever you have on hand. The main ingredient that absolutely must be in stuffing is stale bread. Yes, stale. Of course, you also need a liquid to soften the stale bread. Up-time, they liked to use poultry broth or stock, but we're going to use small beer, since it's easier and cheaper." Elli's love of creating new recipes really shone on episodes where the cook had to make do with whatever was on hand. She had become so popular that she had a contract with the Grantville University Press to write her own cookbook. As profitable as *The Settlement Cook Book of 1903* was for everyone involved, they were all excited to see how Elli's book would do.

Sarah Jane was the up-time presenter again. "I won't lie, we did often include meat in the stuffing, but after extensive conversations with all the down-timers in the club, the up-timers in the club have been convinced of the error of our ways." She gave an oversized wink, making it clear that she was joking. Up-timers who could afford to would definitely continue adding meat to their stuffing.

"Let's get cooking!"

* * *

Bethel hugged her daughter "I'm glad you're spending Christmas with us, not heading to Saxony to be with Matt. Next year, who knows? You two might be on your way to having your own little one!"

"Don't rush it! I'm enjoying all our up-time Christmas stuff while I can. I still miss the Christmas lights. It's getting harder to remember what it was like when everyone had them, but the Hallmark ornaments, and the knock-off Hallmark ornaments, have survived well. Don't tell Dad, but I'm glad the stupid moving reindeer he put out in the yard are gone. I always hated those creepy things. I wish someone had brought back a copy of the Charlie Brown Christmas special, though."

"Yeah, that was a classic. I still feel a knot in my gut thinking about those boxes of glass ornaments I crushed in '32. They were the expensive flocked ones, too. I keep hoping we'll get more tinsel. I should've bought some that year some entrepreneur cut up old mylar balloons for tinsel. Odd tinsel colored on one side, but tinsel nonetheless. Haven't seen it again."

"Is there any particular store you want to stop in first to do your shopping, Mom?"

Bethel looked embarrassed. "Um, well, the new outfit Nils is making me should be ready at Flannery Fashions."

"Really? I love it. You deserve it! They did a great job with the Fourth of July/Grand Opening outfit for you. Is this one for a special event or just a new outfit?"

Now Bethel looked truly, deeply uncomfortable. "Your Dad was invited to a fancy Christmas dinner in Magdeburg with a bunch of muckity-mucks because of his new job, so I need a fancy dress. They took my measurements, and I gave them a budget. I'll be as surprised as you to see what they made, but I'm wearing these old gold pumps with whatever Nils made me." She held up a bag she was carrying and shook it slightly. "I always liked these shoes and only got to wear them twice. Shall we go in and see what Nils made me? Oh my God. I can't believe I'm calling a fashion designer by his first name like I'm the muckity-muck!"

Bethel Ann grinned, open the door wide, then swept her hand to motion her mom inside. "After you, *Frau* Little von Up-Time!"

"Don't sass me girl!"

Nils smiled upon seeing her enter. "Ah, *Frau* Little! A pleasure to see you again! We have your ensemble waiting for you. Krystal helped us pick the fabric and assures us that it's 'very Christmas', so we hope you will be pleased." With a swish, Nils drew aside the curtain to a dressing room so she could see her new outfit.

"It's fabulous! Mom, you are going to be a knock-out in that."

Bethel giggled. "Krystal was right. It *is* very Christmas! A very *up-time* Christmas! Mele Kalikimaka! That fabric must be from Irene's stash, am I right?"

"Krystal and Sam insisted."

Now she outright laughed. "Well, I love it. I never in a million years would have thought of using Hawaiian print for Christmas, but it works. Is that a wrap skirt? The red print skirt looks fabulous with the green velvet sheath dress. That's the part Raymond will like since it shows off my curves without the wrap skirt. I'll be the talk of the party."

"This is indeed the goal." Nils was pleased.

"Now I 'just' need to drag Raymond away from Leahy for long enough to get to the party."

Bethel Ann decided to have some more fun at her mom's expense. "*Frau* von Up-Time! Remember your place! That is a job for Dad's staff, not you. I bet he isn't the only one who will need to be forced to go. The support staffs can all work together to force the senior staff to leave the hospital and go to Magdeburg. I do not envy them that task."

"I know you're joking, at least partly, but you're right. I'll let them take care of getting your dad away from Leahy. I'll spend some extra time with your little brothers before we go. I think Hette has plans to spoil them while we are gone. Every time I talked about taking them along, she told me they wanted to stay home and changed the subject. When I asked them, they said they wanted to stay home."

Bethel Ann shrugged. "You could be reading too much into it. They're all used to Samuel being treated badly outside of Grantville."

✳ ✳ ✳

"I understand what everyone is saying about towns not changing their names. The Holy Roman Empire never allowed it. Having recently visited Narnia, I would like to point out to all the *elected* representatives assembled here that we are no longer part of the Holy Roman Empire, which barely exists anymore. That leaves me with one question: Do we need to bring Princess Kristina into this?" That left the room completely silent. "Motion to accept the request to allow Garnsdorf to rename itself Christmas Town?"

Some abstained, but not a single politician opposed the motion. There was no way Princess Kristina was not going to be excited about Christmas Town. The most realistic of them offered up prayers that she didn't decree that Christmas Town would be ruled by a hereditary Santa Claus instead of a proper mayor. No one who had met the young lady would put it past her.

PART 5: 1635

Bethanne Kim

CHAPTER 14

January 1635 Saalfeld

Johan stretched as he stepped off the train in Saalfeld. "Gisela! You didn't have to come get me yourself. I would've found my way, but it's great to see you."

"Are you kidding? *Mutti* has gone on a mid-winter housecleaning tear now that Christmas is over and before her teach-the-teacher classes are back into full swing. One of her students got stuck in a snowstorm and they are waiting for him to return to resume. Everyone is looking for an excuse to stay out of the new house for a few hours. In fact, I think perhaps we should stop by the shop so you can enjoy a warm bagel and coffee. It's right over there and you can see the facilities in peace and quiet before we go back to the madhouse of our new home."

Johan swung his pack onto his shoulders and sauntered along after her to the small shop *Up-Time Bagels & Cream Cheese* rented near the station. They sat upstairs, in the small meeting room. "Are we really going to do this?"

"We agreed that it's important, Johan, and the up-timers want this to happen. I even figured out a place that works. West Virginia County is out of the question, but we need to stay close to Grantville and Garnsdorf." He shrugged his agreement. That much was obvious. "What do you think of Wittmansgereuth? It's just south of the Ring Wall and halfway between the south and east arms of West Virginia County. Schwarza and Rottenback are the only other places that close and surrounded by West Virginia County without being part of it, and they are the wrong direction for us."

Johan thought about it for a minute. "I like it! We should expand into Schwarza when we can. There should be a market for bagels there, and that could be a second guild location with a master, when we have another. You should know that I talked to my sister about the idea. Sibylle said, 'If you do not make Gisela the first master baker of your new up-timer baking guild, I will make sure you are disowned and can never come home again. I mean that literally.' Then she made me repeat it to be sure I remembered, and then she had me repeat it to her every day until I left to come here, and *then* she made me promise to repeat it to you. So, you have no choice. If you are not the first master baker for our new guild, I will be disowned, unable to ever go home again, and it will be entirely your fault. You can't escape. You're lucky I talked her out of a parade to celebrate the new Guild."

Gisela's horrified expression said it all. "She wouldn't? You wouldn't!"

"You're right, we wouldn't. Not the parade, parades are expensive, but I'm not sure about the disinheriting. After being confronted with a parade in your honor, being the first master doesn't seem so bad, now does it?" Gisela stared daggers at his smug grin. "Now, on to the next item. What will we require of apprentices and journeymen?"

Several hours later, Claudette from the coffee shop came upstairs. "Your shop is closing for the day. Do you wish to leave, or should I tell them you will lock up after yourselves?" Startled to see how late it had gotten while they talked through the details, Gisela started to panic. Claudette gave a low laugh. "Don't worry. Jeremias is waiting downstairs to give you a ride back to the Inn, and we had already sent word so your family isn't worried. Shall I tell him you're on your way down?" Johan and Gisela were already gathering their things and putting on their outdoor gear.

February 1635

"*Herr* Ferrara, I know this is hard and we have everything in writing, but we still need to review all the paperwork. There could be missing or incomplete forms, or missing signatures. Also, there are some things I do not understand so you must help me. Her parents are submitting an obituary you and the deceased approved to the newspaper. Her memorial service will be held at St. Vincent's. I do not know this church. Was it left up-time? Do you have a new location for the memorial service?"

Somehow, Gary looked more pained. "I was sure she had updated everything, but I guess not. St. Vincent de Paul's was renamed St. Mary's years ago when we found out Vincent de Paul is alive in the here-and-now and not yet a saint. The memorial service will be held at St. Mary's with internment to follow immediately."

"This listed cremation, but cremation isn't an option, since it prevents being taken bodily to heaven, so burial will be immediately after the memorial service, as you said. The notes say she wanted to be an 'organ downer.' I understand that her mother is the organist. Can you explain this, please?"

Greg gave a watery grin. "That was a typo, a mistake when they typed everything. It should say organ *donor*. Up-time it meant something different, but Tina wants, wanted, to donate her organs for medical students. As a nurse, she knows, knew, how important studying real organs is for medical students, and how few are willing to donate here-and-now. Her organs can show how diabetes and heart disease impact organs. She wasn't quite willing to donate her whole body for dissection, though, so the family can still go to her grave to remember her. That's her word: remember, not mourn."

The young man was scandalized. "She is having her organs removed before being buried? This is nearly as bad as being cremated! How can she go to heaven in the rapture if her body is desecrated in this manner? Do you *want* her to go to hell?"

Greg wasn't a yeller, but having a bureaucratic weenie accuse him of sending his newly deceased wife to hell for following her wishes to let medical students study her organs? That was going too far. The longer he talked, the louder her got. "You. Will. Not. Judge. Me. You are not God. You are not the Pope. You aren't even a wandering drunk of a priest! Do you think a man cut or blown into pieces in battle is going to hell because his body isn't whole anymore? Or a child crushed beyond recognition by a wagon? How DARE you say my Tina is going to hell for such a selfless act! How DARE you!"

Beulah MacDonald rushed in when she heard the yelling. She addressed the pencil pusher, voice ice-cold. "Leave the papers and get out. Immediately. Come to my office tomorrow morning and we will have a chat." After he left, she sat beside Greg, her voice noticeably warmer. "That was rough. Since no one can do organ transplants anymore, we never even thought about people being organ donors for medical students. It is a solid idea, donating for medical students and physician's studies. I'll talk to the other staff here and in Jena and see if we can turn organ donation into a real program." Sigh. "And we'll have to talk to the priests, pastors, and others to keep them from blowing their stacks. We may need to start with small things like the spleen, appendix, and one kidney, stuff we can live without, so clearly, we can go to heaven without them. First steps, right?"

Beulah flipped through the paperwork. "The notes say she gave the mortician a bag with her burial outfit and a few other things before Christmas, so that should be everything, Greg. I am so, so sorry. I can't change what that idiot said to you, but I'll do my best to make sure that never happens again."

May 1635

Liesl still couldn't believe their luck. The Grantville Cooking Club had built a new house with a large yard on land they bought near Schwarza. The kitchen had the latest conveniences, but they were down-time designed conveniences not up-time ones. Things their students could buy for their own use. Liesl's family had been chosen to live there and be the caretakers. They had even agreed that her

Andres could start a butcher shop on the premises if he did free butchering for the school instead of paying rent. Not just agreed but suggested it! Right now, their first group of students was gathered on the front lawn.

"Welcome! We appreciate you all taking a chance and coming here. You are the very first group to take our new course 'Cooking for Innkeepers'. Most of you were nominated by someone from Grantville who visited your inn and told us that it is cleaner with better quality food than most inns. Our goal is to help you make your inns even better, and to help travelers identify the best inns. When you finish our course successfully, you will be given a plaque you can display at your inn. The plaque alone doesn't mean you are considered a 'GG' or Grantville Gourmet inn, because plaques can be stolen. You, the trained innkeeper, will receive a ring with your name and the name of your inn engraved on the inside. Since we aren't made of money here, it's a simple band, but it's enough.

"You are also what the up-timers call our 'guinea pigs'. You are getting the course for free in exchange for helping us make it better and, hopefully, promoting it to other innkeepers and travelers. Your rooms and experience here should give you a better idea of how to run your inn, up-time style. First and foremost, cleanliness. You will all be taking turns cleaning the house while you are here, including the bathrooms, as part of your training. We do not have an up-time washer and dryer, because they are expensive. We have made arrangements with several manufacturers who are lending us washers, dryers, and a variety of other appliances so you can try using them and, they hope, buy one for your own inn. They are offering discounts to any of our students who buy their goods within six months of taking this course.

"After dinner, we will discuss why you each came here and what you hope to get out of your time here, other than seeing Grantville." From their expressions, that was probably the main thing most of them wanted. "Tomorrow, we will start working on recipes and menus for your inns. For now, please take your things to your rooms and explore the grounds for a few hours." Liesl heaved a massive internal sigh of relief that that was over.

June 1635

Anna Maria gave Bethel a giant hug as she got off the train in Saalfeld. "I hardly got to see you at the wedding, but it was beautiful. Bethel Ann and Matt looked so happy! But how are you and Raymond doing with her moving to Bamberg? Will the pharmacy be okay without her?"

"Yeah, they are happy. She didn't want to say anything, but Bethel Ann's been chafing to move out for a while. Up-time, most of our kids were gone from home for several years by her age. They may not have left town, but they weren't living in their parents' house and working with their dad all day like Bethel Ann was. Up-time, the pharmacy needed two pharmacists, but now it needs one pharmacist and one herbalist. This lets her spread her pharmaceutical skills to another area, so it's for the best. When the job in Bamberg came up, she grabbed it, especially since it's so close to where Matt needs to be. I'm hoping I can convince Raymond to take some time off so we can visit. His assistant was a big help getting him out of the office for the Christmas party, I'm hoping she'll help this time, too."

"Should we expect to open a new bagel shop in Bamberg in the near future?"

"I want to say no, it's too far, but I'm getting the feeling Rachel would like to leave Grantville for a while. Starting a new café might be the perfect distraction for her."

"Distraction? I take it a young man is involved?"

"Of course. A rabbi's son she fancied is to marry someone else. She is heartbroken. So is the rabbi's son, for that matter, but he is determined to follow his family's wishes and not his heart, even in West Virginia. So, leaving will be easier for her. Is there any chance we have a baker with enough skill to start another bakery?"

"It's tough. Gisela and Johan are getting them trained, but it's been less than a year. One of the bakers we inherited with the train station location may be good enough by now, but I have heard Gisela complaining about being short of journeymen. Starting that location in Wittmansgereuth so soon already stretched things too thin. It only has a half menu because they are so short-staffed." Anna Maria sat a bit straighter. "What if Rachel moved to Wittmansgereuth for a few months? She could help get things up and running there, including the new guild, and she's got a talent for finding people to work for us."

Bethel thought for a minute. "I like it. I'll talk to her when I get back." Sigh. "So, no Bamberg for a while after all."

July1635

Newly minted RN Krystal Reed arrived at her Aunt Bethel and Uncle Raymond's house the day after she got back to Grantville for a post-graduation visit. "Johan! This is a surprise. I planned to see you this afternoon, when I visit Sibylle. Why are you here?" He was sitting on the porch with her aunt and uncle.

"He needed to talk to me, and your Aunt Bethel. Since we expected you, we told him to hang out and wait for you." Johan looked decidedly on edge, the exact opposite of someone simply 'hanging out.' He rather abruptly stood and handed her a small gift. Since he still wasn't speaking, Raymond prodded him. "Go on, boy, talk to her. She won't bite."

"Your parents and grandparents remained up-time. Your great-grandparents died." The more Johan talked, the more confused Krystal became. "Your aunt and uncle are the closest adult relatives you have down-time, so I have spoken to them and asked them."

"Asked them...?" Krystal hoped she knew were this was headed, but she didn't want to risk embarrassing herself and having Johan avoid her if she was wrong.

"Asked them permission to formally court you and to become betrothed. If you wish it. Do you wish it?" Krystal leapt into his arms and gave him a kiss that lasted long enough for her aunt and uncle to go inside and shoo her cousins away from the windows.

"I wish it! I definitely wish it!"

✻ ✻ ✻

"I cannot believe we did this." Anna Maria was mentally exhausted from the past year, and beyond ready for a break.

"*We* didn't. *You* did." Dorothea was proud of her new friend.

"Whatever. It is done. The town did what it promised. They built the school. I trained the teachers, and they built the school. I can't believe how much of a ruckus there was over naming the school. I'm supremely relieved that whoever tried to get Kringle Elementary School approved was shot down. That would have been awful! The only thing worse would have been Santa Elementary School. I did like Captain GARS Elementary School a lot, though. That would've been a lot of fun. An easy mascot everyone would want to root for."

"I heard they are thinking of building another school on the other side of Saalfeld, out toward the easternmost end of the county. They want to name that one Captain GARS, but I've heard rumors of a few more schools being started around the county, so they'll have to move quickly to secure the name, especially after we named ours for his daughter." Like most West Virginians, Anna Maria was a huge fan of Princess Kristina and felt a touch possessive at times.

"I heard some people who live in Magdeburg are upset about that. Since she lives there most of the time, they think any school named for her should be there. But our school opened first." They both smiled serenely at the thought of having caused people in the capital city consternation, perhaps even a bit of jealousy.

"Did you know the school had a cement square made with her handprint and footprint to put out front? They want to add a new one every year, at least until she's grown. They got the idea from some famous Hollywood movie theater."

Dorothea was surprised. "Really? How odd. That does sound like an up-time thing." *I wonder if we can do something with that idea in Christmas Town? Hmmm. I'll have to think on that. Up-timers have crazy ideas, but there are so many you can 'take right to the bank'.* "I didn't know Princess Kristina had visited the school already."

"Oh, she didn't. They went to her with a wooden form filled with concrete to press her hand and foot into. Her ladies in waiting were forewarned and made sure she was wearing old shoes. After it dried, they brought the forms here." Anna Maria thought it was a charming way to include the young princess in the school. After four years, she no longer thought about how crazy their ideas could seem.

Thinking back to her years in Grantville, inspiration hit Anna Maria. "Did you know up-timer parents joke that this is 'the most wonderful time of the year' for parents? It's from a Christmas song. That could be a great marketing gimmick for visiting Christmas Town around this time of year!"

September 1635

Linda was nervous. When she decided to do this, almost on a whim, she had expected perhaps a handful of people, but that wasn't what she ended up with. What she ended up with was auditions spread across three weekends to hear everyone and see where they fit; a three-page, double-sided wish list of songs in tiny script from up-timers; and a sudden realization that she needed instruments too, because there was no way this choir was fitting into any church in town. She was kind of wishing she hadn't said "everyone welcome."

"I've never directed a gospel choir before, but my Tina loved them. None of our churches had enough people for a full gospel choir Before, but Grantville has grown a mite over the last few years!" That got the laughter Linda hoped for. "Now, it's finally time to start the rehearsing. We know that some of you will be dropping out for a lot of different reasons, so we aren't even going to try to keep track of who's here for a few weeks. Hopefully you all have heard some gospel already, but you should know there are lots of different kinds. I couldn't find any decent videos of gospel choirs, but a few people had bits and pieces of things like part of a Tammy Faye Baker show at the end of a video, or an ad with a Gospel choir in it, and one of the kids at the high school copied all the bits and pieces together so we can see all of it at once. When the video ends, please leave the auditorium and head out to the football field. Someone else reserved this space, but they agreed to let us watch the video first."

Twenty minutes later, they were reassembled near the football field. "I see we've already lost a few. Gospel singing isn't for everyone, and that's okay. We love having so many people here just to give it a try. We're going to start with one that all the Grantville area churches sang last weekend, so you should be a little familiar with it." As the Grantville Gospel Choir started its first rehearsal, the sounds carried through the high school football field and out into the town.

Swing Low, Sweet Chariot, Comin' for to Carry Me Home....

GRANTVILLE GOURMETS CAST OF CHARACTERS

Agatha Schulte, lives with Sam and Krystal. Finds the sock knitter.

Alyse Ballentine, transplanted Texan and lover of Mexican food.

Andreas Gutmann, husband of Liesl Pfeiffer. Blacksmith.

Annisa Barnes, owner of the Cow Barnes.

Anna Maria Schneider, lives with Sam and Krystal. Teaches crafting classes.

Anna Onofrio, elderly Italian cook.

Augustus "Gus" Heinzerling, priest at St. Mary's Catholic Church.

Balthasar Abrabanel, medical doctor.

Barbara "Grannie B" Albano, grandmother to Bethel Little.

Bernice "Bunny" Lamb, property manager in Grantville.

Bethel Little, co-owner of *Up-Time Bagels & Cream Cheese*.

Bethel Ann Little, daughter of Bethel and Raymond Little. Apprentice pharmacist at Moss and Little Cut-Rate Pharmacy.

Betty Ruth Snodgrass, resident at Bowers Assisted Living Facility.

Beulah MacDonald, Director of Nursing, Leahy Hospital.

Bina Blumenthal, daughter of Cohen and Gabriel Blumenthal.

Brent Little, son of Bethel and Raymond.

Caroline Platzer, principal lady in waiting to Princess Kristina.

Christina Ferrara, daughter of Greg and Tina Ferrara.

Claud "Claudette" Arbaleste, Calvinist and co-owner of Joe's Joe coffee shop.

Corrinne Moss, John Moss' wife.

Dietrich Schulte, son of Heinrich and Anna Maria Schulte.

James Nichols, medical doctor.

Dorothea Bauerin, co-owner of The Inn of Plenty in Garnsdorf.

Elfriede "Effi" Schuetzin, masterful and inventive cook. One of the most popular presenters on the Grantville Cooking Club TV Show.

Eli "Grandpa Eli" Reed, grandfather of Bethel Little.

Erasmus Ebert, co-owner of The Inn of Plenty in Garnsdorf.

Gisela Schulte, lives with Sam and Krystal. Founding baker for the *Up-Time Bagels & Cream Cheese*.

Gottfried von Pappenheim, Bohemian general.

Greg Ferrara, Tina's husband.

Hannah Wiegand, the new cook at Herr Nehring's hunting cottage.

THE GOURMETS OF GRANTVILLE

Hannelore "Hanni" Evertz, wife of Gus Heinzerling

Harry Lynch, the man Anna Onofrio has a crush on.

Heinrich Schulte, woodworker who lives with Sam and Krystal.

Heironymous Cott, property manager in Saalfeld.

Hette Treutmann, widow who befriends Samuel and Julius, then moves to Grantville with them.

Irene Flannery, curmudgeon, crafter, and faithful member of St. Mary's.

James "Jimmy" Ferrara, son of Greg and Tina Ferrara.

Janice Ambler, director of the Cooking Club TV show. High school teacher.

Jeremias Ebert, drives a shuttle between The Inn of Plenty in Garnsdorf and the Saalfeld train station.

Jerry Hart, up-time resident of Grantville.

Jimmy "Dick Head" Dick, owner of multiple local rental properties.

Johan Becker, journeyman baker who moves to Grantville with his sister, Sibylle.

John Moss, apprentice pharmacist and partner in Moss and Little Cut-Rate Pharmacy.

Jost Erhard, tinsmith. Manufacturer of the sock knitter.

Judith Roth, up-time resident of Grantville.

Judith Weymar, terrible cook at Herr Nehring's hunting lodge.

Julie Mackay, organized and ran a Christmas party for the whole town in 1632.

Julius Fruehauf Little, adopted son of Bethel and Raymond Little.

Justin Marbury, Englishman and former nursing student.

241

Kristina Vasa, Swedish Princess and heir to the throne.

Krystal Reed, nursing student. In denial that they are never going back to their former lives.

Lawrence "Larry" Mazzare, Father, Priest at St. Mary's Catholic Church.

Leon Arbaleste, co-owner of Joe's Joe coffee shop.

Liesl Pfeiffer, founding member of the Grantville Cooking Club.

Linda Bartolli, organist at St. Mary's. Founding member of the Grantville Cooking Club.

Lyle Kindred, editor of *The Grantville Times.*

Margaretha Kniess, friend and eventually business partner with Gisela.

Marge Beich, housekeeper.

Mike Stearns, politician.

Morris Roth, jeweler.

Jorgen "Nils" Jorgensen, master tailer at Flannery's Fashions.

Pastor Gregory, finds orphans, including Samuel and Julius, and brings them to places they will be cared for.

Philip Bartolli, co-owner of Bartolli's Surplus and Outdoor Supplies.

Rachel Sagan, researcher. Founding partner in the *Up-Time Bagels & Cream Cheese.*

Raymond Little, pharmacist and Bethel's husband.

Rebecca Abrabanel, Mike Stearns' wife.

Rebecca Cohen, works at the Saalfeld bagel store.

Reverend Jones, pastor in Grantville.

Sam Reed, student. Silent partner in Flannery Fashions.

Samuel Hornung Little, adopted son of Bethel and Raymond Little.

Sarah Jane Mason, cookbook editor for Grantville University Press.

Schmuel 'Samuel' Blumenthal, apprentice bagel baker.

Sibylle Becker, sister of Johan and friend of Krystal.

Thomas Nehring, merchant and owner of a grand hunting lodge.

Tina Ferrara, part time nurse. Terminally ill.

Tyrone Powers, journeyman woodworker.

Ursula Durer, herbalist at Moss and Little Cut Rate Pharmacist.

Werner Wiegand, butler at Herr Nehring's hunting lodge.

Willie Ray Hudson, head of The Grange.

Printed in Great Britain
by Amazon